Other books by Deirdre Hutchins

The Paranormal Investigators League series

(Ghost hunters, anyone?)

PIL #1 Voodoo in Savannah

PIL #2 A Hanging in Tucson

PIL #3 Suicide on Sunset

PIL #4 The Legend of Providence

PIL #5 Darkness in Denver

These are all available from the San Joaquin Valley Press.

Visit us at www.sanjoaquinvalleypress.com

The Dark Prophecy

Book 1: Resurrection of the Vampire

A Novel about Vampires and Witches

By Deirdre Hutchins

San Joaquin Valley Press
Fresno, California

The Dark Prophecy is published by
    San Joaquin Valley Press
    P.O. Box 9485
    Fresno, CA 93792
    www.sanjoaquinvalleypress.com

This is a work of fiction. The characters are not based on any actual persons, living or dead. Any apparent identification with any actual person is purely coincidental.

Cover design by Andria Davis Kaye

ISBN 978-1-7378061-0-3

The Dark Prophecy

Book 1: Resurrection of the Vampire

1

The night was still.

So still you could hear the quietest rustling of leaves gently blowing in the air. The sky was dark, but cloudless. A crescent moon sat nestled in a dark velvet backdrop.

Somewhere in the distance a dog howled—or was it a wolf? Didn't matter. The residents of St. Mary's Cemetery were way beyond worrying about the cries of a lonely wolf. A sea of headstones filled the rolling hills, from gate to gate.

A gust of wind blew a handful of leaves down off an old oak that protected the graves in the back east corner. The leaves rolled over headstones, large and small. Some tombstones were bursting out of the ground, announcing the life and death of their deceased loved ones, while others lay against the grass modestly memorializing the buried ones beneath them.

A mouse scurried across a flat headstone, ignoring the words that told the world that here lay a beloved wife and mother. A leaf blew past the mouse, and they went their separate ways.

The leaf continued to roll, twist and float through St. Mary's, landing on the black boot of a tall man, stepping into the moonlight. The man peered over his shoulder, where the rest of his team was following his act of jumping over the cemetery gate and breaking into the cemetery way past visiting hours.

"He could be anywhere," a woman hissed at the tall man.

He shushed her but otherwise ignored her as he continued looking for the grave he was told to find. He indicated to the team all around him to split up and start looking. They all knew well what they were after.

But St. Mary's was a huge cemetery—they would be looking for a while. Only one person knew exactly where he was buried, and she watched in the shadows, not daring to tip her hand.

"Well, well." Another man with dark skin, clean shaven and impeccably dressed, led a group of half a dozen of his own followers. They had entered through the front gate. They didn't need to sneak around. "A little brazen, don't you think, Ivan?"

The tall man in the dark boots, stood up straight. He had been hoping to go undetected, but this would complicate things. Ivan's team, sensing the impending threat, slowly made their way closer to their leader.

The dark leader of the other group stood on one hip. He wore a long coat and it blew in the breeze, copying the leaves of the oak trees lining the cemetery. He had the look of a man who didn't get his hands dirty. He was confident. He knew his team would be the ones to act, if it came to it.

Ivan didn't respond right away. There wasn't much he could say. They knew why he was here. It was why they were here too.

After a moment or two of silently sizing each other up, the dark man said, "You are out of your territory, Ivan. Leave now, and take your band of

Prudens with you." He spat the word *Prudens* out of his mouth like it was poison, burning his lips and tongue.

Ivan held his hands in the air to show he wasn't here for a fight, although he would fight if he had to. "You know I can't do that, Marcus."

The woman who had earlier complained about how hard it would be to find the grave took a defensive stance and hissed. All around Ivan, his team prepared for the fight they knew was inevitable. They had come for one thing and couldn't leave without him. The future of their tribe was at stake.

The handsome man with the dark skin named Marcus looked at the back of his hand, as if this whole encounter bored him. "You're pretty foolish, you know. To put that much faith in the Prophecy."

He knew he shouldn't be goaded, but Ivan took the bait. "As if you stroll the cemetery every night looking for your next meal."

Marcus smiled, but there was no warmth. It was a cold, heartless grin. "But you see, this is *Bellinz* territory, so I can stroll here as much as I'd like."

Ivan breathed in deep, although his lungs needed no air, and squinted his eyes in anger at Marcus's claim. His voice came out as an inhuman growl. "He's not yours just because he was buried here."

Still sounding calm and bored, Marcus replied, "Nor is he yours. This is your last warning. Leave now."

Ivan crouched into a fighting stance, but the change in his body language was enough of a signal for his female companion. She charged at the woman standing in front of her, extending her fangs and claws as she ran. The Bellinz woman was caught off guard, but she was able to defend herself from teeth sinking into the flesh of her neck. She was not able, however, to stop the claws from gouging her forearms from elbow to wrist.

The fresh scent of blood triggered the others into action.

Both Ivan's Prudens tribe and Marcus's Bellinz tribe ran at one another, claws extended. Neither could back down now. They would kill if they had to, as hard as it might be. Neither side could leave without *him*.

A Prudens man with long brown hair sailing behind him grabbed a Bellinz woman and tore her neck open with his teeth. He spit the foul taste of the rival tribe onto the ground. The woman flinched slightly, but even with her neck wide open she fought back, jumping on the Prudens man with her claws extended. He landed on his back, she on top of him on all fours, claws piercing through his shoulders and pinning him down. She smiled maliciously, her fangs extended. She licked her fangs slowly, as if to relish this moment before the final bite.

Her hesitation was her doom. The Prudens man rolled over as she gloated, knocking her grip loose. She fell backward and all he could reach was her foot, so he grabbed it and twisted it, ripping it clean off from the stump of her leg. Blood swirled around his feet, mixing with the blood of the makeshift battlefield all around him.

Looking around him, the Bellinz woman no longer a threat, he wondered where Ivan was. The moonlight shone on Ivan like a spotlight, and the

Prudens man with the long hair saw his leader locked in a fight he was losing. Two Bellinz warriors flanked him. One clawed at his arms, the other reaching for his neck. Ivan was fast and strong, but he was being doubled up on. The Prudens man walked over to the Bellinz man attacking Ivan's arm and grabbed him from behind. He threw him toward the trees, crashing into a headstone and forcing a large fissure down its middle.

It was the help Ivan needed to block a bite to the neck. The Bellinz warrior bit hard into his arm, shredding the flesh. Ivan gritted his teeth but still managed to growl an order to the man with the long hair. "Find him."

It was all the instruction he needed. With a snarl, he looked back over his shoulder, not a clue which direction to go. Instinct took over and he bolted off toward a dark corner of St. Mary's cemetery.

A Bellinz warrior saw the Prudens man taking off, and he knew he couldn't let him find the boy first. The Bellinz warrior ran as fast as he could, gaining on the Prudens. When he caught up to him, he pounced on the Prudens's back, both of them rolling with the momentum.

In the dark shadows, a girl was watching and she knew the hour had come. She had to resurrect the boy and get him out of here before either of these Tribes laid claim. No one here knew the Prophecy better than she—and she wasn't about to lose everything she'd worked toward.

Running over to the small headstone that read "Shane Walker," she began to dig at the earth as quietly as she could, displacing the grass and dirt. She worked quickly and quietly, glancing over her shoulder every now and then to make sure no one was coming. She *had* to get to him first. Everything depended on that.

She knew she was close when a hand burst forth from the loose dirt. He was alive again. She grabbed his hand and pulled with her superhuman strength, removing dirt as she unearthed him.

And he was just as she remembered him. Sandy blonde hair, greenish-brown eyes so similar to hers, an almost-olive complexion. He blinked the dirt from his eyes, taking in his surroundings. Confusion distorted his face. But when he saw her, he stilled.

"Julianna?" His voice was barely more than a whisper. He couldn't believe his newly resurrected eyes.

He saw the panic reflected on her face as she threw a finger to her lips to silence him. She gestured for him to follow her, and she ran toward the back gate of the cemetery.

Covered in dirt, he tried to stand but his legs gave way. They felt like cooked spaghetti beneath him. As he crumpled back to his grave, Julianna ran back to him, tossing him over her shoulder as if he weighed nothing.

She glanced around once more to make sure she had gone undetected and then bolted, with Shane flopped over her shoulder. As they bounded over the gate in one swift jump, Shane saw the carnage of the battle in St. Mary's below him. It looked like humans, but they didn't fight with weapons. They were ripping into each other with their hands.

"What's going on, Julianna?   Where are you taking me?" Shane asked, pushing up on Julianna's back, her long curly blonde hair cascading all around him and bouncing as they ran.

"Shhhh," was all the answer she would give as she ran further and further into the Santa Monica mountains.

When the graveyard from where he'd been taken was no longer visible in the distance and they were covered by the thickness of trees and tall grass, Shane pushed off Julianna's back, landing on the ground with a thud. She turned to him to grab him again but he scrambled back.

"No." He held up a hand to her and she stared in wonder and terror. She *knew* they would follow. "I want answers, Julianna. How are you alive? Where are you taking me? What's going on?"

Julianna took a step closer, her face softening. The moonlight slipped between the branches of the tree above them dancing across her beautiful face. She was just as he'd last seen her. But how could she be right before him?

"There is only so much I can explain to you right now. You need to feed or you will die. This time forever," Julianna explained.

"Feed?" Shane asked quizzically.

Julianna nodded. "I am not alive. I am reborn. These past five years I've been living as a vampire. And, Shane, you are a vampire too."

Shane wanted to laugh in her face, but suddenly, as if her words were a trigger, he could feel the burn in his throat and he suddenly intensely craved a drink of blood. Before his eyes he saw red and there was a pounding in his ears. He grabbed at his head and shouted, "What's happening to me?"

Gently, Julianna pulled him close to her. "You need to feed."

She was so close and so real. He touched her face. He had missed her so. "Mom and Dad need to see you, Jules. They need to know you're okay."

"My sweet little brother, I'm not okay. To them I am dead. And you are too. You can't see our parents ever again." Julianna's face was soft, sad.

"Were those people in the cemetery vampires too?" Shane asked, suddenly piecing some of the loose ends together in his mind.

"They are." Julianna nodded, helping Shane to his feet, to encourage him onward.

In his mind's eye he saw limbs being ripped off, flesh torn from bone, blood everywhere. "What were they fighting over?"

Julianna hesitated only for a moment. He needed to feed. She had wanted to get him to a city before any of this conversation. But it was too late now.

"*You*, Shane. This is all about you."

2

The waves crashed in the moonlight, pulling back and then crashing again. Glass of wine in hand, Theresa watched the Pacific Ocean intensely. She listened carefully to the comforting sound, letting it overwhelm her senses and wash away any stress she was feeling.

This had always been her favorite time of night. Emily and Kara were tucked carefully in their beds, her role of wife and mother fulfilled successfully for the day. Very few people were out and about. Very few sounds could drown out the nature all around her.

And she loved living in Ventura, California. It had taken her a while to find a home where she truly felt at peace, but now that she'd found it, it meant everything to her. This life felt right.

Her husband, Richard, joined her out on the balcony of their oceanfront home. He slipped his arms around her waist, breathing in her perfume. Theresa smiled to herself. *Dreams do come true.*

Four hundred years ago she'd met her first husband. She'd been naïve back then and married for love. When the bastard—who'd told her he'd loved her over and over—found out she was a witch, he'd turned on her in an instant. She'd felt betrayed, humiliated, angry. And still she'd been heartbroken when she'd had to turn him to dust.

But all these years and thousands of miles later, she'd finally gotten it right.

She'd seen Rich driving around town in his fancy convertible with the top down and she just knew. He was married back then but that was easily dealt with. And then she'd just needed to hex Rich, slipping love potion into his evening nightcap. People were much less worried about witchcraft these days, so he'd never even suspected her for a minute.

And so she slipped effortlessly into the family, in

the process gaining two young daughters.

Emily was sixteen now and not as trusting of Theresa anymore. Perhaps she'd never really been. She was too much like her mother. Sweet. Caring. Always seeing the good in people.

There was no hope for her.

Kara, however, Theresa could see joining the coven one day. She had real potential. And she seemed to love her stepmother. And Theresa had watched her cheat in school, lie to her father, manipulate friends.... Yes, Kara would be a great witch one day.

Theresa turned around, wrapping her arms around her husband's neck. He was handsome, rich, successful. She wasn't really in love with him, but she was in love with the life he gave her. So it wasn't that hard to smile and pretend to be interested.

They were both still dressed from the day. Theresa in a simple floral-patterned dress, her brown hair piled high upon her head. Rich wore his suit from the office, but the top button was now undone and the tie loose around his neck. She leaned in and kissed his neck. He groaned, pulling her closer. She pulled on his tie, kissing up his neck, standing on her tiptoes to reach his jawline. Just a hint of five-o-clock shadow was starting to appear. In the moonlight, he looked more rugged, more Theresa's type.

Never one for foreplay, Rich unzipped her dress and kissed her savagely, taking control of the moment.

And then her phone rang.

"Don't answer it," Rich encouraged, his lips still plastered to hers.

Pretending it was hard to resist his charms, she pulled back slowly. "I have to. It could be work."

The phone was on the patio table. She glanced and saw the name. Elyse. Yes, this was the call she'd been waiting for. She let Rich remove her dress completely and continue kissing her neck while she answered.

"This is Theresa." She forced herself to sound cheery, even though her heart was pounding in her chest. Only not for the reason Rich suspected.

"It's time," Elyse said cryptically into the phone.

"Oh really? An emergency? And it can't wait until tomorrow?" Theresa piled it on thick, glancing back at Rich. He was focused on her body, not her words.

"Get to the meeting place as fast as you can. He is risen. The countdown has begun." Elyse delivered the message and then the call ended.

Rich unclasped her bra and then she berated herself for not slipping him a sleeping potion. But how could she have known tonight would be the night?

She turned around and took a giant step away, clutching her bra over her breasts. "I'm so sorry honey. I have to get to the salon immediately."

He looked hurt, confused. "Now? At 11 pm? What salon emergency could there possibly be?"

Damn. She'd known this day would come all this time and still she was unprepared for everything. Think fast, Theresa. "Pipe burst. Water is everywhere. I have to meet the department of water and power."

"Can't someone else take care of it?" Rich stepped toward her.

She stepped back into her dress and turned for him to zip her up. "It's *my* salon, Rich. *Our* money."

He slipped his arms around her one more time. "We have plenty of money. Just give me fifteen more minutes."

Fifteen minutes? Yep, that was about right. A war played inside Theresa's mind. If she gave Rich what he wanted, she could leave in peace and focus on the issue at hand. But time was of the essence with the Dark Prophecy, and the first to move would have the upper hand.

Fifty years ago, she wouldn't have cared so much. Let the damned bloodsuckers kill themselves off fighting over their precious prophecy. She hated those vile creatures anyway. But now.... She turned and looked into Richard's eyes, hearing the ocean waves behind her.

Now she had everything to lose.

She seductively pulled her still unzipped dress down slowly over her shoulders. A smile danced across Rich's lips.

First Richard, then vampires.

And she would bring a fight they couldn't win, even with their golden resurrected boy.

3

Shane followed his sister and peered around the building. His throat burned. His legs felt shaky beneath him. He was so weak. He had never thought much about the reality of vampires during his short human life. And now he believed he was one. He had never wanted anything more in his life than to rip open someone's neck and feast on their insides.

And the thought didn't sicken him in the least. In fact, it excited him.

"Bars are the best," Julianna said, teaching her brother. "You can always find at least one person who wanders off on their own, stumbling drunk. They won't even know what's happening."

He knew he should listen to Julianna, to wait for her instruction. But his sensitive ears heard the voices.

His sensitive nose could smell their flesh from a block away. The *thump, thump* of their heartbeats called to him.

"Wait till one of them separates from the group," Julianna instructed from over her shoulder, but it was too late. Shane had already bolted at lightning quick speed toward the three drunk patrons leaving the bar. "Oh no."

Julianna followed her brother and saw that he'd already selected a victim, a young girl with a beret. Who wears a beret these days? Some artsy person, she supposed. Shane had already sunk his fangs into her neck and was gulping down her blood. The artsy girl was wide-eyed, but she hadn't even screamed.

Her two friends, however, were witnessing, and Julianna had a responsibility to her younger brother. Besides, she was thirsty too.

Her first thought was to get the whole scene out of the street and away from the streetlights. At this point it was still possible that anyone witnessing from their windows might think Shane was kissing the young girl's neck, but as the life force left the artsy girl's body that would be harder to believe.

One gentleman in a turtleneck and one lady in a crocheted dress remained, watching their friend's attack. The gentleman turned to run. The lady started to scream. *Fight or flight*, thought Julianna. You never really know who you'll be until the moment comes. Julianna expected that Turtleneck imagined himself as the one to defend his lady-friend's honor. To draw his sword and duel. But when the vampires actually struck, he ran like a little bitch.

Shane kept gulping behind her as Julianna grabbed the back of Turtleneck's shirt. With superhuman strength she threw him into the alley down the side of the bar, away from streetlights. She then cut off Crochet's scream with a twist of her neck. She tossed her body into the alley next to Turtleneck. He was dazed but scared. No doubt he'd be trying to run again soon.

"Your next lesson will be about discretion, Shane," Julianna whispered to her brother with a smirk across her lips. She pulled him and his artsy victim into the darkness of the alley. And then she turned to Turtleneck. He was sobbing, staring at Crochet's lifeless body. The reality of what was happening to him had apparently started to settle in.

"Please. I beg you. Die like a man." Julianna was sick of his whimpering. She watched as he stood up and ran—again—down the alley away from her. She could see as clearly in the dark as if it were day, so as he ran deeper down the unlit alley, Julianna only sighed. She could see what he could not. There was no way out.

In what for Julianna was a light jog, she caught up to Turtleneck and ripped his stupid shirt from his body, exposing his chest and pulsing neck. He was breathing heavily and his heart was pounding. The aroma was intoxicating. Normally, Julianna would take the time to savor her meal, but she knew Shane had quite the head start on her, and she was afraid of what he might do after his first meal. Some newborns relished the kill. Some moped with the guilt that comes from taking their first human life. She had no way to know which way Shane would lean.

As quickly as she could, she extended her fangs and sunk them deep into Turtleneck's neck, holding him tight against her. He struggled a bit at first, still trying to run. But eventually he stopped struggling and she continued to drain his body of blood. She couldn't leave any victims.

When there was no more to drink, she carried Turtleneck's lifeless body back to Crochet's body and where she'd left her brother with his victim.

Shane sat up against the brick wall of the alley, the lifeless girl at his feet. His mouth, his chin and the front of his shirt were completely covered in blood.

Julianna shook her head. "Discretion *and* manners. No one would ever suspect you won the fight, Shane."

She extended her hand to him to help him up and encourage him on. They needed to clean up their mess and keep moving. But Shane knocked her hand away. By the scowl on his face, she assumed he was struggling with killing the artsy young girl.

"You'll get used to it, Shane. We don't have time to mope." Julianna looked over her shoulder as if someone might appear. "You had to get your first feed in, but they could be here any moment."

"Exactly." Shane looked up at her, his face dark and brooding.

She didn't understand. "Grab your kill and get up. We have to keep moving."

"No." He leaned his head back against the alley wall, resting his hand on his one bent knee. "I want answers. I'm not going any further until I get them."

"Our tribe leader, Lord Dimas, will tell you everything. I promise," Julianna pleaded with him. "I'm taking you to him as fast as I can."

He turned toward her. He looked fierce. He was so much older than when she'd died. He'd been only fifteen at the time. At that time, her little brother had still been growing, just starting to fill out and change from boy to man. But now, before her sat a very intimidating vampire. She had to remind herself that he was the one from the Prophecy and that he would be the most powerful of all.

She crouched down on her haunches in front of him. "I'll tell you what I can quickly, but then we need to keep moving." She ran a hand over her thick blond curls. "Vampires have been fighting for centuries in what we call the Shadow Wars. There is a prophecy, known as the Dark Prophecy, that a vampire will be born who will end the fighting and unite us all. You are the one. The vampire from the Prophecy. That's why everyone wants you. They want you to join their tribe so they can be the ruling class of vampires when the Shadow Wars end."

Shane was silent for a moment, considering her words. Then he laughed. Julianna watched him toss his head back and laugh hard, almost hysterical. He was still laughing and shaking his head when he responded, "That's ridiculous."

She looked again outside the alley. They really didn't have time for this. She had carefully mapped out the whole thing—his death, his resurrection, his first feed, and then everything would be revealed by Lord

Dimas. Shane's stubbornness had not been taken into account. She was getting nervous and angry. "What exactly is so ridiculous? The Bellinz and Prudens tribes from the cemetery will be here any minute."

Shane shrugged. "So? They won't hurt me. You said so yourself. I am *the one*." He laughed again.

Julianna stood up, tired of her brother's attitude. "You have to get to Lord Dimas. He knows the Prophecy better than anyone. He'll explain everything. You'll see." She picked up Turtleneck's body again. "Now grab your kill so we can hit the road."

Shane grabbed her hand. Hard. She stared at his grip. He was very strong. "Who turned me?"

Julianna stared back into the eyes so like her own. Regardless of Shadow Wars and vampires, he was her baby brother. They had played together as children. She had lied to her parents for him. "I did."

Shane froze, trying to process her words.

Julianna continued. "We're members of the Strashni tribe. Remember that. If anyone tries to convince you to be open to other tribes. You are

Strashni."

"I'm not part of your little politics," Shane spat back at his sister.

Julianna shook free of his grip, resisting the urge to hug him. "You are, Shane. No matter what you do or where you go, the Dark Prophecy will follow. Lord Dimas will train you. Come on."

She picked up Crochet's body, tossing Turtleneck's body over one shoulder and Crochet over the other, leaving Shane's artsy victim for him to carry. A glance back over her shoulder in the dark alley revealed her brother, standing now, the moonlight shining directly on him. It struck her as powerful, as if all of nature knew his importance.

His voice was small and his eyes soft. "Why?" He cleared his throat. "Why did you turn me into a monster?"

Again she realized that she had carefully thought through every detail *except* Shane's reactions. She stepped toward him. "This was always who you were meant to be. I knew it from the moment I first heard the Prophecy. If it hadn't been me, it would have been someone else who turned you. And I didn't want you to wake from your resurrection and see anyone else but me." He may not understand today, but he would in time. If there was one thing Julianna knew with all her heart, it was that.

"Five years ago? When you died?" Shane asked the question that had been burning in his heart since the day he stood at her graveside service with the rain gently falling all around him.

Julianna closed her eyes. She hadn't been prepared to get into *any* of this with him. "A Strashni warrior had seen me working at the diner. He had thought I had good potential, so he turned me." She stepped again toward her brother. "Please understand. As a human, I was dead. I couldn't go back. I couldn't explain."

Shane shook his head. "I don't understand any of this. I'm just a regular guy. I'm not the savior of all vampires. Jules. You made a really big mistake."

They stared at each other in the moonlight.

Julianna struggled with what to say to get him to go to Lord Dimas. Dimas would make everything all right, just like he always did. They were running out of time.

"Shane, I can only promise you that Lord Dimas will explain everything. But we have to go now." She gestured her head out toward the streets. "We have to clean up these bodies and get to Dimas."

Her brother seemed sad as he effortlessly lifted his first kill, tossing the body over his shoulder just as he'd seen Julianna do.

Julianna ached to be the one to convince her brother, but there was so much to tell, and every tiny moment could possibly push this all spiraling in the wrong direction. "I don't regret becoming a vampire. My life with the Strashni is more than I could have ever dreamed it would be. I know with every fiber of my being that this is what I was meant to be. And I know with every fiber of my being that you *are* the one from the Prophecy. You'll be the greatest vampire ever to roam the earth. And I'll be with you every step of the way."

Whether he believed her or not, he was at least moving, stepping toward her. "Let's go."

With a smile of relief, Julianna stepped out of the alley into the streets. Her plan had been to dump the bodies in the mountains, where authorities would come to the conclusion they'd been hiking and attacked by wild animals.

But they'd run out of time.

Under the haze of a streetlight, Marcus stood with his hands folded near his hips, his long coat blowing in the wind. He was surrounded by three Bellinz vampires. *I guess we know who won the fight in St. Mary's Cemetery.* He sneered at Julianna and the sandy blonde vampire standing right behind her.

"Well, well. What have we here?" Marcus stood up straight, not a scratch on him from the fight earlier, his clothes as perfect as they'd been hours ago.

Shane stepped around his sister to get a better look at the vampires who were after him. What did that even mean?

Julianna dropped the two bodies she was

holding right there on the street and leaned into Shane whispering, "Run."

And she bolted at vampire speed, back toward the mountains. She expected her brother to follow her. By the time she realized she had failed to predict her brother's state of mind yet again, it was too late.

She was alone. And Shane was captured by a rival tribe.

4

Theresa stepped into the darkness of her salon and then locked the door behind her. When she had convinced Rich to buy this place for her, she knew it was the perfect cover-up for her coven gatherings. In the front, a normal salon. A place for mani-pedis, chairs for haircuts and styling. No one who worked here suspected anything of the warehouse out back. She cut through the salon and opened the door to the warehouse. If Rich had ever wondered why she'd needed a sizable warehouse for a salon, he'd never voiced it.

But it was perfect. The warehouse was tucked in back with a side entrance the witches could use to come and go, and it was large enough to hold their ceremonies and meetings. She walked through the red door and entered the warehouse, where Elyse met her instantly.

"What took you so long? Everyone is panicking." Elyse spoke softly but her words were laced with concern. Theresa loved Elyse. She had handpicked her to become a witch and the de facto second in command, but she didn't care for insubordination.

"The meeting starts when I get here." Theresa leaned an inch from Elyse's face, the challenge clear on her face.

Elyse looked to the ground. She knew perfectly well that Theresa was far more powerful than she. Compared to Theresa, Elyse was a baby. She'd only regenerated a handful of times.

With strong powerful strides, Theresa began to walk to the center of the warehouse, where she could see twenty of her Harbor Coven witches. But Elyse gently grabbed her arm, leaning in to say, "*He's* here."

Theresa snorted. He had better make this worth her time.

"Gather, witches." Theresa stood in the center

of the circle of witches, her arms extended, her voice commanding. "I hear we have a visitor."

Stepping out from the shadows behind a pile of boxes, stood the nameless vampire who had been feeding her with information. In exchange, she'd provided powerful potions filled with strength, power and protection. He was clearly a piece of shit, selling out his own kind. Theresa barely trusted him. But so far his information had proven to be useful.

"Your majesty." He bowed deeply. Theresa wasn't really a queen, but she never corrected him because she liked the show of respect. She was just the leader of the Harbor Coven, a coven she had built with her own hard work and grit.

"Do you bring me news of the Prophecy?" Theresa held her head high, her palms at the ready. She could shoot him with electricity if he tried anything funny.

"I do." The vampire stood tall. He was handsome for a bloodsucker. Theresa imagined he was able to lure lots of victims with his good looks. "The vampire from the Dark Prophecy has been resurrected. He is held at the Bellinz compound. If you wanted to kill him, now would be the time."

Theresa knew very little of the Prophecy, only that a powerful vampire would be born. As she understood it, most vampires were excited by his arrival. Why did this one want her to kill him? She *did* want to kill him, but she didn't want to be used as this asshole's pawn.

She played it cool. Theresa had lived through many major historical events by keeping a level head and never tipping her hand. She smiled. "Thank you for your information, as always." She turned to her Number Two. "Elyse, give him the regeneration potion."

Elyse hesitated. This would give this bloodsucker a second lease on life if anyone tried to kill him. But Theresa was her leader and so she only hesitated for a second. She also didn't want to find out what happened when you annoyed Theresa twice in one evening.

She handed the mysterious vampire the potion,

avoiding looking into his evil face. He disgusted her. "Drink this standing directly in the moonlight. It will protect you from death for five years."

His evil grin gave her the chills. And then he turned, exiting out the side door, slinking into the night like the rat he was. The witches watched him leave in silence.

"Are we killing the vampire from the Prophecy?" a soft voice asked from the ring of the circle. Theresa turned to see a pretty young witch named Camilla. She had soft brown hair that bounced across her shoulders. Camilla had been another selection by Theresa. Her innocent beauty made her the perfect poisonous flower. She could easily become a very powerful witch if she stayed close and learned everything she could from Theresa. Her natural proclivity to the potion arts was already becoming evident.

"We might. But I don't want to play into that two-faced vampire's hands," Theresa explained. Her coven was her family. She knew she could speak openly to them.

"We are a powerful coven, but we're not very big," Elyse said, adding her opinion. "I'm afraid of what would happen if we took on the entire race of vampires."

The witches all whispered amongst themselves, some agreeing with Elyse, some disagreeing.

Theresa silenced her coven with a raise of her hand. "Elyse is right. We don't need to start a war. But I would like to send a message. Who would like to visit the Bellinz compound with me?"

"You know I always serve you," Elyse answered. A few other witches also nodded in agreement.

"Perfect. We'll leave just before dawn, when vampires are at their most vulnerable." Theresa smiled wickedly. "And now we should do the Midnight Dance, to prepare for whatever may come."

"Theresa?" It was Camilla's soft voice again. "What happens to us? If the Dark Prophecy comes true?"

Theresa's eyes narrowed. "It is a vampire's prophecy. It never mentions us."

"But you must have a thought about how it would affect us?" Elyse added.

Theresa looked around the witches' circle. They all looked worried, staring at her for guidance and salvation. She would burn every vampire in her wake before she'd let everything fall apart. She had the most to lose of all.

"The vampire from the Prophecy is supposed to unite all the tribes, which would of course, make them all the more powerful," Theresa explained to the Harbor Coven. "But I will never let those monsters destroy what we've created. Yes, there are more of them than there are of us. But they have a mere fraction of the power we have. They're monsters. We're spiritual creatures."

The faces all around her softened.

"And what of the two-timer?" Elyse asked her mentor.

Theresa shook her head. He was playing some kind of dangerous game, and she would have to figure it out to make sure she wasn't tricked into doing something she didn't want to do. But if she was smart, he would get what was coming to him from his own kind. "I think we let that scum orchestrate his own demise. If the bloodsuckers ever found out what he was up to, they'd take matters into their own hands." She smiled at all the precious witches surrounding her in a circle. "It would be a shame if someone were to ever let that information slip."

Wicked glee danced across the faces of the Harbor Coven. Only Elyse, uneasy from the magic she'd provided the betrayer, dared to ask, "But we gave him potion to protect him for five years?"

Theresa walked to her precious Elyse and put a comforting arm around her shoulders. She was only sixty, still such an infant in the world of the immortal. She would have to teach her about the treachery of honesty. "My dear Elyse. I myself prepared that potion." Elyse just looked at her, waiting for more of an explanation. So Theresa continued. "So perhaps the ingredients were merely couscous, rosemary and water."

A small smile spread across Elyse's lips as the realization dawned on her. The witches in the circle began to cackle all around her, the wickedest, loveliest sound in the whole world.

"The two-timing bastard will now think he's invincible." Theresa couldn't suppress the amusement her trick provided her. The witches continued laughing all around her. Trickery was one of their favorite pastimes. But tricking a vampire was the ultimate satisfaction.

Theresa licked her lips with evil glee. *Game on, you bloodsucking asshole.*

5

Marcus got great joy out of shoving Shane into the Bellinz compound. Although there was no need. Shane had come completely willingly.

The only moment's hesitation Shane had had was the shock at seeing where the vampires lived.

In movies, they were always holed up in dark, cobweb-ridden castles. This was a beautiful two-story mansion where the backyard was a sandy beach. The style was modern with decorative stones adorning the front wall from grass to rooftop. There was a balcony on the second story, and tall, arching windows that seemed to cover the house.

And when Shane stumbled through the large, double front doors, he was surprised again.

Lights were on everywhere. They were soft

lights, as if they were on a dimmer, but it definitely didn't feel like the inside of a den of vampires.

"Follow me," Marcus instructed, his long coat flapping around his legs. He held his head high, walking with purpose. If he wasn't the leader of the tribe, he had to be pretty high up there. He had such an authoritative presence. And he was so classy. Shane found that he really liked him. He followed him without hesitation.

Marcus walked up to a lady who appeared to be about thirty years old. She had thick black hair falling softly on her shoulders. Her long muscular legs were crossed. The fingernails at the end of her long, slender fingers were painted a bright red. The shade matched her full, thick lips.

"My queen." Marcus lifted her hand and kissed it reverently.

She allowed Marcus his respect, but she didn't return the attention. Her eyes were drilling into Shane. He stood taller under her scrutinizing gaze. He assumed everyone had some expectation of the vampire from the Prophecy, but he could only be what he was. Somehow it still made him a bit self-conscious.

"So, you are the one." She remained sitting on the barstool, a glass filled with red liquid in a wine glass. Shane knew it was blood. He could smell it from where he was. Somehow, she still looked like a queen on her throne, even though it was a barstool in a beach house. She was so regal, her dark eyes so piercing. Shrewd.

Shane didn't know what to say, so he answered, "That's what they keep telling me."

The queen laughed heartily and stood, walking with her hips swaying until she was uncomfortably close to him. He stood his ground, unsure of her motives. When she was an inch from his face, she leaned into his neck and sucked in through her nose, drinking in his scent.

She moved her face back to be in line with his, her lips so close to his they grazed. "I'm Regina, leader of the Bellinz tribe. Welcome to my home." And then she kissed him, allowing her teeth to bite on his bottom lip and pull it toward her.

Then she smiled and backed away. Shane felt

more confused than anything. When she was again seated on her barstool throne, he asked, "Why am I here?"

She lifted her glass and took a drink of the thick, red liquid. She slowly licked her lips and then smiled. Shane could feel his own throat beginning to itch again. Regina answered, "You're my guest."

"I was told every tribe would want me," Shane said, cutting straight to the chase. The confusion and the lack of information were grating on his nerves.

"Shhhh." She shooed her hand in front of her face as if his questions were annoying her. "Let's not talk business. Marcus will get you someone to drink on." She gestured at Marcus, and he bowed regally and left the room. "Come. Sit next to me and let's get to know one another."

She tapped the barstool next to her and he hesitated for a moment. Perhaps he should have listened to Julianna. He knew nothing about being a vampire. Deciding it was best to not have enemies, he sat on the barstool.

"Your name, please." It was an instruction.

"Shane Walker." He cleared his throat. Why was she making him nervous? Perhaps because she looked at him like a wolf looked at a bunny rabbit.

"And who resurrected you?" Her thick, gorgeous lips were pursed in front of him.

"Julianna. My sister." He decided he had better not keep information that soon everyone would likely know anyway.

Regina didn't seem to like the answer. She hissed and pulled away. "Dimas's girl."

Shane swallowed hard. He didn't like the idea of this Lord Dimas being the possessor of his sister.

Regina leaned back in the barstool, feigning relaxation, but Shane could sense her tension as thick as a wire. "I was born two hundred and twenty-four years ago right here in California. My parents were Catholic. Perhaps that was why they could sense my maker's evil. I was naïve, I guess." She shrugged, as if it were all no big deal how she went from wholesome Catholic girl to vicious monster. "He told me he loved me and I interpreted that as we would get married, have babies, own a rancho."

She leaned forward, again uncomfortably close to Shane, her elbows resting on her knees, her full bosom peeking out of her dress. "Instead, he ripped my throat out and forced me to drink his blood with my last dying breath. I resurrected two days later and drank both my parents dry."

She sat back all the way and lifted her wine glass, swirling the red liquid. The coppery scent of blood wafted from the cup and tickled his nose. She continued her origin story. "His name was Adolfo, the leader at that time of the Bellinz tribe. I joined him at his side, and we fought for years for our territory. The Prudens have wanted the beachfront for centuries. Assholes."

Shane shook his head. His voice soft, he asked, "Why are you telling me all this?"

"I believe in you, Shane Walker. I believe that you will end the Shadow Wars, stop the senseless battles that took my Adolfo from me." Her eyes began to shimmer ever so slightly. "Vampires are killing vampires. And it isn't right."

She put her hand on his knee, pleading in her eyes. He was moved by her story, but he had no clue what it was she wanted him to do.

The silence between them hung heavy and thick as Marcus entered the room again with a teenaged girl in tow. She was pale, eyes sunken. Human but not afraid inside this vampire compound.

"Ah, good choice, Marcus." Regina reached for the young girl. "This is Marissa. She's one of our feeders. She lives here rent free and we care for her in exchange for her blood."

Marissa stepped forward and extended her wrist to Shane with a small smile. He could see the scars of multiple bite marks. He could hear her pulse calling to him, see the veins bursting beneath the skin. Nature took over and he extended his fangs, sinking them into her wrist. She didn't even flinch as he sucked her blood from her body.

"Don't kill her though, Shane," Regina

instructed. "I know you're a newborn, but good feeders are hard to find." Regina sat back on her barstool and crossed her long legs again.

Her words shook him from his reverie, and he withdrew his fangs, sitting straight up. Blood trickled down his chin and he remembered what Julianna had said earlier about the way he ate. He looked down at the dried blood on the front of his shirt.

"That's normal," Regina explained as if she could read Shane's thoughts.

Marissa ran her finger along Shane's chin, wiping up her own blood and then sticking it into his mouth. He sucked her finger, resisting the urge to bite her again.

Marcus remained standing, but Marissa withdrew her finger, bowed and then left the room. Shane licked his lips.

"The Strashni will undoubtedly come for you." Regina stared at Shane, taking in his wild, sandy blonde hair, his Southern California style. Again, he had the feeling she could see straight to his soul. "What will you do then?"

"What do you mean?" Shane was so confused. He felt like he was thrown into a maze where the only directions were provided in dizzying riddles.

"You came here when you could have fled with your maker. Your sister." Regina bounced her leg in front of her. "You didn't know us, so you didn't choose us. But you didn't choose Strashni either. Why not? Most vampires join the tribe that resurrects them."

Shane knew he liked Marcus. He was finding a soft spot for Regina too. She was...intoxicating. And without his sister, he felt very alone in a world he didn't know how to belong in. He decided to shoot straight. If he really was the one, they would have no reason to want to hurt him, would they? "I don't know anything about anything. What's a Strashni? What's a Bellinz? Hell, what's the damned Prophecy even? I'm told I'm the key to this Prophecy and I'm going to unite vampires, but all I know is one moment I am living the life of a twenty-year-old man and the next I'm dead with a craving for human blood."

"Undead," Marcus responded. "We prefer the term undead."

"Fine, undead." Shane shook his head. "I don't know. I don't understand. Why me?"

Regina stood, extending her arms. Shane stepped into her embrace. It felt good. Motherly. She held him tight, even rubbing his back. When he pulled away, she tousled his hair like a mother would do. "No one knows more about the Dark Prophecy than Dimas. He found it centuries ago. If Dimas's girl believed you were the one from the Prophecy, then it is likely true."

Shane looked up into Regina's dark eyes. She continued, cupping his chin. "You don't have to be a monster, Shane Walker. Yes, this is a new world for you. But you can choose to live it however you like. Especially you."

Regina leaned in again and kissed Shane. He kissed her back, but it felt weird. She was kissing him passionately and he looked at her like a mother figure. She pushed him back into the barstool and climbed on his lap, pulling his bloody shirt up over his head and throwing it to the ground. She ran a hand seductively over his chest, desire burning in her eyes. She used her long tongue to caress his neck. She didn't seem to care at all that Marcus stood a foot away, watching the scene unfold.

With his shirt off, Shane sobered a bit to the moment. He realized this was going in a very different direction than he'd expected. He decided to stand and push gently away from Regina. "Look, I don't want you to get the wrong idea. You're a beautiful woman, but I don't exactly see you that way."

Regina's eyes narrowed. Her uncanny perceptions were on the mark again and she was insulted by his rejection. Her voice was low but laced with anger as through gritted teeth she said, "Then you can spend the day in the bonus room considering what you are giving up. You could fight at my side, just as Adolfo once did. I could teach you everything." She stepped close to him and whispered, "The Shadow Wars are a game, Shane. You'll need powerful allies to win. And I'm an experienced lover."

Swinging her hips, she walked over to the staircase and began ascending.

Marcus grinned, his hands still folded. "Come. Let me show you to your room."

6

"This is a dungeon," Shane said to Marcus as he locked the cage after throwing Shane inside. Marcus only laughed as he left the room.

They had gone down to a lower floor, a basement perhaps, and into what must be called the bonus room. But really it held a giant steel cage, like one that would be used to lock up wild animals.

Beyond the cage there was a couch and TV mounted to the wall in one corner of the room. Unlike the floor above which was well lit with light bulbs, this room danced with the soft glow of several candles. There were no lights down here and no windows either. The lack of windows Shane figured was a good thing. The coming day would be his first as a vampire and he didn't yet know what to expect. He suspected sunlight wouldn't be pleasant.

"Let me guess, she tried to wrap her legs around you and you spurned her advances?"

Shane jumped at the sound of the man's voice. He had no idea someone else was in there with him. Shane turned and saw a man in the darkness of the back corner of the cage, his feet extended in front of him, crossed at the ankles.

"How'd you know?" he asked the stranger.

"I slept with her once," the stranger said from the shadows, not moving a muscle. "Biggest mistake of my life. Now every time she sees me, she tries to rape me, and when I say no, she throws me in here. Crazy bitch never learns no means no."

Shane thought about this and wondered if he would meet the same fate every time his path crossed Regina's in the future. He shook the cage door. It didn't budge.

"Why'd you say no?" the stranger asked. "She's sexy as hell. And I can smell you're a newborn. Why not give in to her advances?"

Shane dropped down to a seated position. The hard ground of the cage was so uncomfortable beneath his butt. "I don't know. She just kinda reminded me of my mom."

The stranger laughed hard and loud. "I bet she really loved hearing that. You'll be down here for years."

"No, the Strashni are coming for me." Shane remembered Regina saying that and he did believe it was true. There were too many tribes out there looking for him to remain hidden for too long.

The stranger groaned loudly and dramatically. "I hate the Strashni."

"What tribe are you?" Shane asked.

"Tribeless. I'm a lover, not a fighter."

Shane hadn't even considered the possibility of being tribeless. "I didn't know that was a choice."

"They resurrect you, they brainwash you, they make you fight in their senseless war. I chose a different path. I said 'to hell with it all' and struck off on my own."

"Supposedly I can't do that." Shane looked

through the cage bars at the room around him. Perhaps this was the best place for him to be. No one expected anything of him in here. "Everyone keeps telling me that I have to unite all the vampires."

The stranger stood in one quick movement. This was the first time he'd even seemed alive. "What did you say?"

Shane sighed. Perhaps he shouldn't have said anything. It had been nice for a moment just being another guy. In prison. "I guess there's some prophecy out there that says a vampire will be born who will unite all the vampires. I never really got the details. I was supposed to learn everything from Lord Dimas, but I never made it that far."

"*Lord* Dimas?!" The stranger stepped out of the shadows allowing the candlelight to make his features glow. He was movie star handsome, like someone who would play a chiseled superhero. Every hair in place, the angles of his face flawless, his body tall, lean and muscular. "He's calling himself a lord now?"

"You know him?" Shane asked. He supposed the

vampire world was much smaller than he gave it credit for.

"I knew him. Years ago. We were young vampires together. He's a dumbass. And the reason I hate the Strashni," the stranger answered, his face reflecting thoughts of years gone by.

"Well, I'm told he knows everything about the Prophecy and he was supposed to explain why it all points to me." Shane stood up and began inspecting the lock. "I guess I gotta get to him if I want answers."

The stranger walked over to the front of the cage and leaned against the bars, crossing his feet at his ankles. "I never believed in the Prophecy. To be honest, I always thought *Lord* Dumbass just made it all up."

Shane stopped looking at the lock and stood up, looking the handsome stranger right in the eyes. "Really?"

"Makes more sense to me than some all-powerful vampire uniting a bunch of self-centered piece-of-shit monsters," the stranger said, shrugging.

Shane thought about it and his shoulders

slumped. It actually *did* make more sense than the idea of him being the all-powerful one they were talking about. "Then I guess everyone's making a big fuss about me for no reason."

"Sometimes they just need something to believe in. Is it so awful that it's you?" The stranger extended his hand. "By the way, I'm Luke."

"Shane." They shook hands.

"May I ask where your shirt is, Shane?" the handsome stranger named Luke said, eying his bare chest.

Shane looked down and then up at Luke. He smiled a little half-smile. "Collateral damage. She got it off before I fully realized what she wanted."

Luke smiled back. "Well, I'm glad you didn't let her have her way. It's nice to have someone to talk to."

The bonus room door opened and in walked a vampire Shane had yet to meet. He handed them each a container like a re-usable water bottle through the cage bars, and then left the same way he'd come in.

Luke unscrewed the cap hungrily, drinking like

he'd been left in a desert to die, the excess dripping down his neck and onto his shirt. Shane slowly unscrewed his container and sniffed. It was the foulest scented thing he'd ever smelled. If food had been left to rot in the sun and roaches were buried in it, it would smell better than what they had handed him in this container. He gagged.

"Pig's blood," Luke explained. "We'll see if you're so picky in a few days."

Shane screwed back on the cap and placed his container down in the corner. Thanks to Marissa, he wasn't that hungry. "How long have you been down here?"

Luke shrugged after he wiped his mouth with the back of his wrist. "Lost track of time. Maybe six months?"

"Six months?!" Shane staggered at the thought. He couldn't go six months without answers.

Luke looked around the room and then at his newfound companion. "You know, you're not what I would've expected."

Shane looked up at Luke. "I thought you didn't believe in the Prophecy."

"I don't, but if I did, the vampire savior would be warrior-like. Strong, rugged. You look like a surfer."

"I *am* a surfer." Shane grabbed the cage bars. "Look, it doesn't seem right to me either."

"How'd you end up in Regina's clutches?" Luke stepped forward and pointed at Shane's container of untouched pig's blood. Shane took a step back, insinuating that Luke could help himself.

While Luke devoured his second cup of the foul blood, Shane thought about the bizarre night he'd had. "Well, I had just had my first kill." He remembered what Julianna had called it and he wanted to use the right lingo. "And then these Bellinz warriors were standing there. I was supposed to run and meet up with Lord Dimas, but I don't know. I was curious, I guess."

Luke smiled, showing teeth glazed with red from the pig's blood. "You didn't want to run from a candy ass like Marcus, dressed like a male model and filing his nails. I get it."

"And I wanted to understand. Everyone's fighting over me because I am some powerful chosen one, but it makes no sense. I'm just me." Shane shrugged.

"There's one way to find out." Luke turned to face the room, grabbing the bars just as Shane did. "So, the vampire of the Prophecy is supposed to be all-powerful and shit. Meaning he can control the elements."

"What does that mean?" Shane asked.

"I guess it means he can control air, water, earth, and fire," Luke answered. "So if you can control the flames of those candles over there, then you're the one from the Prophecy. If not," he shrugged, "then it's a crock of horse shit."

Shane looked at the flames. They moved like magic, big then small, up then down, the firelight casting strange shadows around the room. Could he control the flames? It seemed ridiculous. "How do I do that?"

"How the hell should I know? I'm not the chosen one." Luke gestured to the flames. "Just be one with the flames or something. Call to them."

Shane thought about it. If he really tried and nothing came of it, at least he could stop wondering. Having no clue what to do to control the elements, he closed his eyes and felt for the flame. His fingers tingled and energy rose around him. Somewhere across the room he could feel the pull of the fire. He went with it.

He extended his fingers and a zap snapped from the flame to his fingertips.

Luke watched as the flame shot across the room like a small fireball, extinguishing when it got to Shane.

He and Shane exchanged a look of pure surprise.

Luke shook his head and laughed. "Well, ain't that a son-of-a-bitch. You just controlled fire."

"I did?"

"Yeah. It flew from over there to your fingertips. Do it again," Luke instructed his new friend.

Again, Shane closed his eyes and focused on the flame. This time when he felt its pull, he opened his eyes and watched a small ball of flame race toward him. When it made it to his hands, he held it there like a baseball. No pain. No heat. He was mesmerized and confused at the same time.

Luke slapped him on his back. "So maybe a small part of the Prophecy isn't completely a bunch of bullshit after all. You're controlling one of the elements."

Shane looked from the fireball to Luke. "What exactly does it mean?" This didn't mean that the Prophecy was true, did it? And that he might actually be worthy of everything they'd been saying? It made no sense.

Luke flashed his handsome smile. He'd been around for centuries and the one thing he'd learned in his undead lifetime was that it was good to have friends in high places. He was happy to have met this newborn surfing vampire. "At the very least it means you are going to be one very powerful vampire."

"Just because I can make a fireball?" Shane asked. He was still struggling to comprehend what it meant—if it even meant anything at all.

"I realize you are a young vamp," Luke went

back to sitting on the floor, extending his feet in front of him in the same position he'd been in when Shane had also been thrown into the cage. "But vampires are many things. They are fast, strong, powerful. Some can even rip your limbs off with their bare hands. And I've seen many amazing things in my time. But I've never *ever* seen a vampire hold a ball of fire. Chosen one or not—you, my friend, are very special."

7

"That's where they're holding him, Elias. I'm sure of it." Julianna stood under a tree, hiding in the shadows. The sun had not yet risen, but it was teasing a peek behind the mountains. She only had a little time left to rescue her brother.

Elias peered over her shoulder, across the two-lane highway that ran along the beach in a huge arc around the Bellinz beach compound. "How can you be sure?" The words 'since you ran' were implied but not said.

Elias was a Strashni warrior. His long, black hair slicked back and his tall, muscular body reminded Julianna of a Native American. With some war paint, she could imagine Elias riding a horse and shouting a war cry. Three other Strashni warriors crowded in around them, trying to see the compound, but Julianna knew Elias was the best and so trusted him the most. This was more than saving her brother on a rescue mission. The entire Prophecy depended on this moment.

Julianna raised her nose to the air and dragged in a deep breath. As clear as day she could smell her brother's scent. "He's in there. I don't know where he is being kept or what they're doing to him, but he's in there."

"If they believe in the Prophecy, he's probably being crowned their king," Dorian, a blonde warrior, snarled in her ear.

Elias shook his head, his long black hair swaying with the movement. "Regina would never relinquish control. She'll try to manipulate him."

"The plan is to go in and out as quietly as possible. Ideally, we'll be completely undetected. Sneak in, get Shane, leave." Julianna looked up at Elias. He looked angry and ready to fight. "No fighting unless we have to. All we need to do is rescue Shane."

"Can I please kill just one? I hate the Bellinz

vampires," Elias snarled.

Julianna thought about it. She hated the Bellinz too. All her life as a vampire they had been trying to poach Strashni territory. And they were so damned prissy. And now, they'd kidnapped her brother right from under her nose. That bastard Marcus knew damn well she had resurrected Shane. And he stole him anyway. "Fine. Kill some Bellinz. But please be discreet."

Elias nodded. He was an amazing assassin, so she knew vampires would die tonight without even knowing what had hit them.

From the shadows, Julianna surveyed the compound before using her gift of keen vampire sight. There were two warrior vampires flanking the front door and she could see vampires pacing in the front windows. On the back balcony, she caught a glimpse of another vampire. But along the side of the beach house, there was no protection. "There. We'll enter through that side door."

Elias, Dorian and the other vampires would

follow her lead. They were soldiers, not captains. And this was her mission. Besides, she was Dimas's right hand so they would do whatever she said. Slowly she crept down from the hill and out from the protection of the trees. The tiniest sliver of sunlight crept over the mountain behind her and scorched her back. But she powered through it, her Strashni team behind her.

Nothing mattered but getting to Shane. And quickly before sunrise.

They crossed the highway and then ducked into the cover of the bushes on the side of the Bellinz compound. A twig snapped beneath Julianna's foot and she froze, listening for any reaction, watching for the vampire at the back of the house to come investigate. While she was looking around, she caught sight of four figures in long hooded robes. They were coming in from the beach, as if they had manifested in the ocean. Their heads were held high, as if they had no reason to sneak—or, more likely, sneaking was beneath them.

Julianna let out a deep, guttural growl, the urge to rip something to shreds almost overcoming her senses. "Witches."

Elias watched the figures head toward the side door they had planned to use. If the vampire at the back of the house saw them, he did nothing. Or, Elias suspected, they had hexed him. "What the fuck are they doing here?"

She had no idea how she knew it, but she knew it deep in her bones. These witches were after Shane.

†††

Regina heard a crash somewhere in the house and she sat straight up in bed, letting her exposed breasts bounce freely beneath her. She couldn't care less who saw her naked body, least of all Marcus, who was naked beside her. He'd been her boy toy for centuries.

"What was that?" Regina asked slowly, carefully. She didn't want to overreact, that wasn't her style, but she had precious cargo in her stronghold and she didn't want to lose it before she'd secured his alliance. Perhaps she had been a bit sensitive when he had spurned her advances earlier, but she'd always enjoyed teaching men lessons. A few months in her bonus room and he'd be begging for her body. She was a master at using her feminine curves to get men to do her bidding.

Unless he was gay. Damn. That hadn't occurred to her earlier. She may have to see if he had a better reaction to Marcus. It would change her plan a bit, but it could still work.

"Someone probably knocked over a lamp in their feeding frenzy, my Queen. I'm sure it is nothing." Marcus stroked her arm, trying to coax her to finish what she'd started.

She leaned in and kissed him passionately. "I'm sure you're right," she said with a wicked grin. "But still, I think you should confirm that, Marcus. Go find the source of the crash."

Marcus rolled away from Regina and she watched his strong, lean back muscles ripple under his dark, mocha-colored skin as he climbed out of her bed and put his black pants back on. He didn't bother with his shirt. Over his shoulder he smiled back at her. "Back in a minute. Wait for me."

Another loud crash and the sound of people yelling sobered them both into action. Regina jumped out of bed grabbing for the red silk robe that lay near her bed. Marcus had already bolted out the door and down the hall.

†††

"Don't kill any vampires. We can't be sure which one he is," Theresa instructed her witches. They stood at the side door of the Bellinz compound, the shadows of an almost-rising sun just beginning to form. Their black hooded capes helped hide their faces. "I just want to give him a message."

Elyse and the others nodded to their coven leader.

Theresa held her hand up to the door, palm out, and it opened on its own. She crept in first, looking in every direction. She was surprised to see no one guarding this door. "Spread out and find him. Remember, don't kill."

"How do we know when we find him, Theresa? The informant was vague on details," Elyse asked from the darkness of her hood.

"He's the most powerful of all vampires. I imagine we'll know quite easily," Theresa answered, but the truth was she wasn't exactly sure herself. She only came here to give a message so she wasn't very worried about it. But if she could find him, if she could know who he was...that would be very powerful information for the next time.

All four witches were inside the dark side hallway when Julianna burst through the door. She snarled at the witches, trying desperately not to kill them all.

Elias stepped up behind her and whispered, "Discretion, Julianna. Those were your words. In and out, undetected."

The witches, as calm as ever, watched the internal discussion the vampires were having. Theresa stepped forward, saying calmly and plainly, "Yes, *Julianna*, you should listen to your friend. Discretion."

Something snapped inside Julianna. She crouched down low, growling as she did, her claws and fangs extended. Theresa really didn't have time for this, but she enjoyed playing with vampires. Julianna ran at full speed in the tiny hallway, leaping toward Theresa. And, with a sigh, Theresa flicked her wrist and Julianna flew against the wall, crashing into a decorative vase that had been centered on a small stand.

Julianna's blood boiled. She sprang to her feet, eyes on Theresa, calculating her next move. She wanted her blood, but how to get around her witchy spells.

"Ahem." Elias cleared his throat in Julianna's ear.

"What?" she snapped, but as she turned toward Elias, she saw the answer to her own question. Two Bellinz vampires stood at the top of the stairs at the end of the hallway.

"Strashni," the Bellinz on the left snarled.

Rival vampires at one end. Witches at the other.

"Shit," Julianna muttered.

But Dorian didn't seem to care about the

witches. He ran toward the Bellinz vampires, leaping like a cat toward the vampire closest to him. He knocked him to the ground and sunk his fangs deep into his victim's flesh. The other vampire turned to pull Dorian off his comrade and in the process scratched his claws all down Dorian's back, ripping his skin from his bones. Dorian's shirt instantly turned a deep red, but Dorian didn't stop tearing into the vampire beneath him.

Calmly, Elias walked up to the vampire who had scratched Dorian and lifted him like a rag doll. With one swift move, he twisted the Bellinz vampire's neck clean off, removing his head from the stump of his body. Then Elias leaned down to Dorian and whispered, "The plan was discretion. Why is no one following the plan?"

With crazed eyes, Dorian looked up at Elias and then back down to the vampire beneath him. Then he bit into the vampire's neck and with his teeth did what Elias had done with his hands—he bit the vampire's head clean off. He sat up and wiped the blood dripping down his chin with the back of his hand. He smiled up at Elias, and then Elias offered Dorian his hand, helping him to his feet.

And then five more Bellinz vampires came hurtling down the stairs.

Elias and Dorian, like the warriors they were, crouched in preparation for the attack. One of the Bellinz vampires leapt from the top of the stairs, forcing Dorian backward into the hallway. The other four Bellinz vampires fought Elias and the other three Strashni—limbs, claws and blood splattering everywhere in the tiny hall.

And Julianna watched and knew this was her chance. Hoping the witches wouldn't pay attention to her with the fighting all around them, Julianna slowly snuck toward the descending stairs at the other end of the hallway, following her brother's scent. She slipped away as Elias ripped the arm of his attacker clean from his body, the blood splattering across his face.

"I'm following the blonde. She knows something," Theresa instructed Elyse and the other witches. "You three stick to the plan. We meet back at the Salon when we're done."

†††

"So I'll call Diego in here and tell him I'm still hungry. When he's close enough, you toss a firebomb at him and I'll grab the keys. Then, we escape!" Luke explained his plan to Shane.

"A firebomb? Don't get ahead of yourself. I've pulled a couple of sparks. That's about it." Shane shook his head.

"You just need some more practice," Luke encouraged. He snapped his fingers. "I got it. I'll call Marcus down here and you can use him for fireball target practice. And he has keys too, so if he goes down...win, win." Luke was grinning widely, his fangs starting to show.

"I don't want to practice on Marcus. I like him." Shane grabbed the bars of the cage and shook them again, as if mere force of will could open the door and set them free.

Luke stared at Shane incredulously. "Marcus?

The nice man who locked you in this cage?"

Shane turned back to Luke, his head cocked to the side. "Because Regina told him to."

"But let me guess. You like her too?" Luke shook his head at Shane's naivete. "They're all blood-sucking monsters. Instead of uniting the tribes you should eradicate them."

"What? You're a vampire too."

"Yeah? Well, I hate us all." Luke pointed back at the candles lit around the room. "But right now what I want is to get out of this mind-numbing cage. Start working those 'chosen one' gifts."

Shane just looked at Luke and smiled.

Luke became uncomfortable under Shane's expression. He felt as if he were the butt of some joke he hadn't understood. "What?"

"You're a believer in the Prophecy now, huh?" Shane still smiled at his new friend.

"Not so much a believer, as impressed by your talents," Luke said cautiously. "Okay, fine. Controlling fire is pretty compelling. Now use it for some good and get us the hell outta here."

"I do want to talk to Regina before we leave this place. And then I'm going straight to Lord Dimas," Shane announced.

"Are you insane? No Regina. She'll just rape you. And if she knew about your little fire talents, she'd do even worse. And you shouldn't talk to Dimas, either. He's worse than she is." Luke folded his arms, eyes narrowing.

"She's not going to rape me. And you can't blame her for being a bit lonely. The love of her life died in the Shadow Wars." Shane remembered her sullen face as she'd told him of her past.

But Luke just laughed. "Is that the crock of shit she whipped up for you? *She* murdered Adolfo. She wanted to control the tribe." Luke grabbed Shane's shoulders. "Listen, you're young. I know this is all new to you. But if you're going to rule over vampires one day, the first lesson you have to learn is that we're all monsters. Now get us out of here with your firepower, try not to get raped on the way out, and we'll figure out the next steps at that point."

"Are we becoming a tribe?" Shane asked with a smirk.

Luke shoved Shane's shoulder. "Get us out of here."

"Fine." Shane closed his eyes and concentrated on all the flames in the room. If he called all the fire, perhaps he could form a large enough ball.

"Woo," Luke shouted like a cowboy at the rodeo.

Shane opened his eyes and glowered at Luke. "You broke my concentration."

Luke shoved Shane's head to force him to look at his own hand. A ball, larger than the last, sat glowing in his hand. "Now throw it."

Shane looked around. Without an escape route, he really didn't want to set the room on fire. The only choice was in the cage. It was metal, so wouldn't go up in flames. He hoped.

As if it were a baseball, Shane wound up and threw the fireball to the back corner where Luke had been sitting when they'd first met. It lit up for a brief second or two and then burned out.

"Yes!" Luke pumped his fist and Shane laughed, proud of his ability. But their celebration was short-lived. They heard a crash in the hallway and then the sound of some sort of scuffle. Shane and Luke exchanged a glance. The fear in Luke's eyes told Shane all he needed to know.

"Diego!" Shane shouted, clutching the bars.

"Diego, we're hungry! Come quick," Luke echoed, rattling the bars of the cage.

"Diego! We need more pig's blood!" Shane shouted. They both shook the cage, making as much noise as possible with the hope that Luke's plan would work before whatever was going on out there got to them. They were sitting ducks in this cage.

The door creaked open slowly and Luke and Shane both stopped shouting. Shane got his hands ready to create a fireball. They waited silently.

And Julianna walked in, holding Diego's head by his hair, his body nowhere to be seen. "Diego won't be joining us today." She dropped the head and it landed with a plunk before rolling across the floor.

Shane was surprised that he didn't even care about the sight of a decapitated head. But he was happy to see his sister.

"Oh, Julianna, it's you. Grab the keys from Diego's belt and get us out of here," Shane explained. He shook the bars one more time for good measure.

"How are you a newborn and yet you already know everyone?" Luke stared wide-eyed between Shane and the blonde vampire rescuing them.

"She's my sister. The Strashni who turned me." Shane looked at Luke as if he were an idiot.

Julianna looked up under hooded eyes at her brother's handsome cell mate as she fumbled with the keys to set them free.

"No. There's no way you and she are related. She's like a goddess." Luke clutched the bars, leaning forward so his face peeked through.

Shane grabbed Luke's arm and yanked him back from the bars. "I said she's my sister. Get that look off your face."

But Luke kept staring at Julianna, flashing his movie-star smile and she returned his smile, stealing glances in between unlocking the cage. When she'd successfully found the key, turned it and swung the door open, Shane bounded out purposefully. Luke stopped at the cage door and grabbed Julianna's hand.

"Enchanté, ma cherie." And he kissed the back of her hand. She giggled.

Shane looked back at Luke and Julianna, his hands on his hips. "Remember, get out and don't get raped. That's the plan. Let's go."

"Don't get raped?" Julianna asked.

"It's a long story." Luke kissed her hand again.

"Come on. We've got to hurry. There are only minutes left before sunrise," Julianna instructed, a nervous edge to her voice.

Shane started briskly walking to the door Julianna had come through. And then he stopped.

Julianna instinctively jumped in front of her brother to protect him, jerking away from Luke in the process. She crouched and hissed, prepared to fight.

Shane only stared at the woman in front of him in the black hooded cape.

"I only want to talk," the woman explained.

"Bullshit. You're here for Shane," Julianna spit back.

"If I wanted Shane, I would have manifested down here, cloaked with invisibility, and murdered him while he's still a baby. I'm just here to talk."

"Who are you?" Shane asked confidently. He stood tall, bare chest jutting out. Julianna noticed he seemed more confident than when she'd left him to Marcus. That Shane had been dazed and confused, and she silently chastised herself for the thousandth time for misjudging that situation so badly.

But gently, Shane grabbed his sister's shoulders and put her to one side. He wasn't afraid of the witch at all. Julianna, however, stayed coiled and at the ready. In time, she knew her brother wouldn't need any protection, but he was still young and untrained. And she was still his big sister.

The woman pulled down her hood, revealing

her beautiful face and brown hair piled high on her head. "My name is Theresa. I lead the Harbor Coven based not too far from here. I care nothing for your little prophecy. I'm a witch, not a vampire, and so have my own politics to deal with."

"Okay. Then why are you here?" Shane asked again, his voice strong. Julianna stood straight at Shane's side, the tone of his voice telling her he didn't completely need her protection anymore. Luke stepped to Shane's other side.

Theresa smiled. "There is a betrayer amongst you. He comes to me sometimes with information about vampire dealings in exchange for powerful spells. You should watch your back."

"You didn't come here to give us a warning, witch," Luke responded, his arms folded across his strong chest.

Theresa's smile grew. "Astute vampires. How refreshing. And you're right. I was hoping for an alliance."

Julianna crouched again, hissing as she did, her

long, thick blonde curls bouncing in front of her shoulders. "We don't make alliances with witches."

Theresa turned to Julianna. "You are not the most powerful vampire in the room. You're not even the most powerful *being* in the room. A new day is dawning. I think we can all agree to that." She turned back to the young, bare-chested blonde vampire before her. "Think about it, Shane. Think of the power with both our forces combined."

"Never," Julianna hissed.

"I'll think about it. You have my word," Shane responded. Julianna glared at him. And then Theresa disappeared, evaporating into a blur and then nothingness right before their eyes.

"That was...hot," Luke said after a moment.

"Shane! You don't know them yet. You shouldn't have promised them anything," Julianna screeched at her brother. He would be hard to protect if he kept making deals with the devil.

"I only promised I'd think about it," Shane replied calmly. "Now let's get out of here before Marcus locks all three of us in the cage."

"*Marcus* put you in there? What was he thinking?" Julianna's shock was written on her face.

"Oh, he wouldn't have been in there long. Regina just wanted him to regret not sleeping with her," Luke explained.

"I'm sorry. What?" Julianna still stood there, confused.

"I'll tell you everything when you tell me everything." Shane stared her down with a strong look that shook her. He'd been on his own for only one night, and already he was starting to come into his own. "Now let's get out of here."

Shane grabbed Julianna's hand and ran out the door Theresa had been standing in a moment ago. Luke followed closely behind Julianna.

"There's a side door. Up those stairs and on the right," Julianna instructed, gesturing the way she'd come. They could still hear the sounds of fighting up ahead.

Shane climbed the stairs cautiously, not sure of

what he'd find when he reached the scuffle. At the top of the stairs, he followed the natural curve of the hallway and saw vampires ripping and biting, blood everywhere. He watched a ribbon of blood slowly make its way, winding and twisting toward him, seeping into the carpet and staining the floor at his feet.

"Dorian!" Julianna's scream alerted Shane to the gravity of the situation. He had no way of knowing who was friend and who was foe, but Julianna's fear told him a Strashni was in peril. He looked up in time to watch a blonde vampire warrior have his head bit clean off. Dorian's head rolled toward them and Julianna screamed, kneeling down to his severed head.

We're all blood-sucking monsters. Luke's words echoed inside Shane's head. He looked up at the carnage before him and impulsively knew what he wanted to do. "Which ones are we?" he asked Julianna.

Her eyes were wild with hysteria, but she pointed at three vampires all losing their fights. "The outnumbered ones."

Shane took a deep breath and closed his eyes. He

raised his arms and shot fire from his hands. Straight lines of fire shot to every Bellinz warrior, burning them to the bone. Their bodies lit up the hallway with the blaze of their burning flesh. The bloodied Strashni vampires backed up, barely singed. The Bellinz vampires burned until there was only a pile of ash where each had once stood attacking a Strashni.

Julianna could only stare wordlessly. She had heard the stories, known the power he would have. But seeing it was a strong dose of reality—and shock at how far he'd come in the one night they were apart. Emotion stole the words from her throat. Dorian's head at her feet left her devastated. And her brother's complete destruction of the Bellinz vampires in one raise of his arms filled her with wonder.

What a night.

Elias walked over to Shane. His shirt was bloody and torn, a large gash ran across his torso, but all his limbs were intact, so he was one of the lucky ones. "What just happened?"

Shane's bare chest was rising and falling. It was

hard to explain something so instinctive. Luckily, he didn't have to.

Luke said, "Oh yeah. Shane can control fire. We hadn't mentioned that yet."

Elias knelt down on one knee before Shane, and the other two remaining Strashni warriors followed suit. "My Lord. I pledge my reborn life in service to you."

And Julianna watched, both thrilled and exhilarated. She had known he was the one. She had known it from the moment she'd heard the Prophecy. And now it was validated. No one could doubt it.

Shane would one day rule them all. And this was barely the beginning.

8

Lord Dimas sat in the darkness of his basement. Sunlight from the dawning day was creeping in through the tiny window, but it was easy enough to avoid. He was growing impatient waiting for news from Elias and Julianna, two of his favorites. He'd trusted them with one of the most important missions they'd ever had.

The basement was barren of furniture. A pool table, small couch, a couple bean bags. He'd kept it this way strategically. He never wanted anyone to get too comfortable down here when he wanted time to himself.

Lord Dimas was tall and lanky. He wasn't a warrior; he was an intellectual. He had been even in human life. His hair was longer than he wanted it to be, straight and white. His skin pale white, making his blue eyes glow by comparison. He wasn't classically handsome, but his features were striking enough that some found him good-looking in an exotic way.

He drank a swig of human blood mixed with a shot of bourbon from a small glass. And he paced again, wondering why they hadn't returned.

When he'd joined the Strashni two-hundred and fifty years ago, he'd thought they were all brawn and no brain. His first fifty years he'd been somewhat miserable. But the thought of being tribeless scared him even more. This was a thankless life where someone was always trying to kill you or steal from you. You had to be shrewd.

It was his cleverness that had won him leadership over the Strashni. And with him as their Lord, Strashni power and territory had grown. With the strength of the Strashni warriors and his intellect, they were unsurpassed by other measly tribes. Regina and her band of whores. Damian and his pack of whiners. Johann and his impulsive brats.

He hated them all and couldn't wait to crush

them.   He imagined his hands on their throats, squeezing until their heads were removed from their bodies. He imagined it so fervently that the glass he was holding shattered in his hands, spilling its contents all over the throw rug beneath his feet. A shard of glass had sliced his hand and he watched the blood drip from his wound, joining the stain on the rug below. Then he licked his hand slowly, savoring the taste of even his own blood.

Dimas sat down on the only couch in the room, ignoring the glass and blood on the floor. He could bide his time. He always had. Like a snake hiding in the grass watching his prey and waiting for the perfect time to strike. Resting his fingers on his chin, he reminisced about the early days as a Strashni, when Lord Mikhail had ruled over them.

What a braggart that guy had been. What an ass.

Mikhail had been a warrior's warrior through and through. He liked to fight regardless of the occasion. It hadn't been hard to win his trust through acts of loyalty. If you did what he said without dissention, you were in his inner circle. Dimas bowed his head to Mikhail for a century without question, weaseling his way into a top position.

Then, when the time was right, he struck him down.

Dimas had made a pact with a small band of tribeless vampires living in the mountains: all the protection of the tribe if they killed Mikhail in his death sleep. Pretending there was a threat to their territory in the mountains, Dimas lured Mikhail and his top soldiers into the trap. They went with bravado, ready to strike down their enemies. They found nothing during the night and Dimas talked them into bunkering down in a nearby cave for the day, since they'd never make it back to the compound before the sun burnt them to a crisp.

Foolishly trusting Dimas with their lives, they left him awake as lookout. When the Strashni were deep in death sleep, Dimas gave the signal to his cohorts—a howl like a wolf's cry. They heard it, they slaughtered, they appointed Dimas the new Lord.

No other Strashni had ever questioned any of the events of that night. Attacked by an enemy wanting their territory was as normal as the moon in a night sky. And after centuries of waiting, Dimas had become Lord.

Yes, he knew how to wait for good things to come.

Footsteps on the stairs that led to the basement alerted Dimas to an impending arrival. He looked up. If it wasn't Elias and Julianna, he would send them away. He only wanted news of the resurrection, not the petty worries of beefed-up warriors.

He let a slow smile of relief creep across his lips when he saw the bounce of Julianna's blonde curls.

"My Lord." She practically skipped over to Dimas, kissing his hand. She had always been true to Dimas, completely enamored by everything he said and did. He loved this about her. And clearly the night had gone well. Julianna's emotions were always on full display. "I was right. I was right all along. My brother *is* the vampire from the Prophecy."

Her eyes glowed with joy and pride. He could

see on her face that she had a tale to tell. He looked around her and raised an eyebrow at the bare-chested vampire and the old comrade standing in the doorway near Elias.

"Shane, this is Lord Dimas. He rules the Strashni and can answer all your questions about the Prophecy." She turned back to Dimas, yanking on his hand to encourage him to stand. "My Lord, I want you to meet my brother, Shane. The most powerful vampire who will ever live."

Dimas wanted to laugh. The boy she believed was "the one" looked like a lost teenager. He had a long way to go before he could even think about calling himself powerful. But she was right that no one knew the Prophecy as he did, so Dimas had to play his cards right.

"Shane. It is beyond an honor to welcome you to the Strashni," Dimas beamed, plastering joy—no matter how forced—across his face. He glanced at Luke but said nothing before looking away.

"I'm looking for information about the

Prophecy," Shane stated.

Dimas didn't really care for Shane's blunt tone. It reminded him too much of Mikhail. "Julianna, you really should offer your brother some clothes. A bare chest and the pants from his death suit? This isn't how we treat our newborns."

Julianna bowed her head, a little deflated from her previous elation. "My apologies, Lord Dimas. So much has happened tonight."

"Lord Dimas." Elias stepped forward, his strong presence filling the room. "I can substantiate Julianna's claims. Shane is already *very* powerful. The Prophecy has begun."

These words struck Dimas in the heart. Julianna was emotional with a flair for the dramatic. She had decided her brother was the chosen one five years ago when she first heard the Prophecy and had never let go of that belief. But Elias, on the other hand...Elias wasn't one to jump to conclusions. "And you know this because...?"

"He burned every Bellinz vampire we were

battling. Burnt them to a crisp with only his bare hands." Elias's eyes were wide as he recounted the moment he'd been saved. "Shane controls fire."

It was only an instant, but Dimas had shown surprise—maybe even fear? He recovered quickly, grabbing Shane's hands and welcoming him into the basement. "Well, then Julianna was as visionary as you are powerful. Please come in."

"Will you tell me everything you know about the Prophecy?" Shane asked as he followed Dimas to the couch. They all paused a moment at the broken glass and blood on the floor, but Dimas offered no explanation so no one said anything. If Shane hadn't been laser-focused on the Prophecy, he might have asked more questions. Not just about the blood on the floor but even how they got blood to put in glasses in the first place. Regina had been drinking it the same way.

"I will." Dimas sat back on the couch and crossed his legs. "And then when I am done, I want you to let me know if you believe you are the one as fervently as Julianna does." Elias, Julianna and Luke remained standing, facing the couch watching Shane and Dimas.

Shane nodded to Dimas, both to confirm that he would be honest and to urge Dimas to continue.

"Our kind was formed through a curse hundreds of years ago. Vlad the Impaler was cursed for his bloodthirstiness. He spilled more blood as a human than many of us will ever spill as a vampire. And with this curse, he became a child of the night with a craving for blood." Dimas leaned his hands on his chin, his voice melodious and smooth. Shane watched intently. Even Julianna, who had heard this story dozens of times, never tired of hearing Dimas tell it.

"He learned that by forcing a human to drink his cursed blood he could pass the curse on to others. At first, he was thinking he would create an army, but it really ended up being more of a family. Anyway, the moral of the story is that we aren't just bloodthirsty for humans. We are wired for violence and power, just as our creator was."

"Get to the Prophecy," Luke said, rolling his eyes.

Dimas shot him a look of pure hatred. "Why are you even here, Lucas?"

"He's here with me," Shane answered, staring from Dimas to Luke. What had passed between these two? The hatred was virtually palpable. "And please continue to the Prophecy and what this all has to do with me."

Dimas sighed. "In the early days, the one who cursed us also spoke of a vampire who would one day unite all vampires and create peace. He claimed a seer had seen the whole thing in a vision, and that this savior would be the most powerful vampire of us all. The legend was passed down on parchment, but also orally, and became known as the Dark Prophecy."

"What does 'most powerful' mean? Controlling fire?" Shane asked.

Lord Dimas shrugged. "It doesn't give that kind of detail. Just that he would be the most powerful. Over the years, people have simply filled in details on their own." He waved his hand in the air as if the things people said about the Prophecy were a gnat he could swat away. "Just rumors. Don't listen to them."

Shane looked back at Luke, who was standing with his arms folded and a complete poker face across his handsome, chiseled features.

"How do I fit into this? From what you've said so far, anyone could be that vampire," Shane stated.

"Ah, yes. On this the Prophecy is quite detailed, so we would all know when he was re-born." Dimas leaned forward. "Unassuming, fair. Noble and rare. As human, a boy with the wind in his hair. Parents, good teachers. A shock to the heart. Never recover when both children part. The century turns, no one will rest. Reborn in spring, he'll rise in the west. When power comes, you'll see his worst. This is the promise: a gift to the curse."

The words hung for a moment before Shane shook his head. "I still don't get it."

Julianna ran to him, carefully sidestepping the glass shards on the rug. "Wind in his hair? You're a surfer! A gift to the curse? Your name, Shane, means gift. And our parents were teachers who buried both their children."

Shane stared at Julianna, lips so taut they twitched. And then he stood, towering over her. He was angry but controlled. Through pursed lips he spoke. "*You* killed me. *You* did this to our parents. It wasn't some accident. And all because of some silly nursery rhyme that makes no sense!"

Julianna shook her head, her eyes welling with the emotion she was trying not to show. "No. I was right, Shane. It's you. The Dark Prophecy foretold of your rebirth and power. How could you doubt it after what happened at the Bellinz compound?"

Shane was silent for a moment. Everyone was watching him. He could see that Julianna and Elias were fervent in their belief in him. The dots weren't connecting for Shane, however. He was just a boy. An ordinary boy. And none of this made any sense. "How do you know these words?" And as he said this, his stare shot daggers at Lord Dimas.

Lord Dimas hated to be stared down. He stood to match Shane's gaze. "No one knows where the original parchment is—probably at Vlad the Impaler's castle. But centuries ago I stumbled across a copy. I have studied it for years."

"Show me." Shane's words were an order.

Lord Dimas was starting a slow boil in his anger. Shane wasn't a ruler of any vampires. Not yet anyway. He was just a newborn and Dimas was still a Lord. He opened his mouth to retort, then thought better of it. Slow and patient. He would stick to what had always worked. "In good time." He smiled, but it was neither warm nor filled with kindness.

Shane was confused and angry, but he didn't think he'd get much more out of Dimas. After staring at Dimas' cold expression for a moment or two, he left the room in a swirl of emotion.

Julianna turned her attention to her Lord and protector. Grabbing his hands she said, "You can help him, right? Train him until he comes into his power fully?"

She looked up at Lord Dimas with hopeful eyes. Her love and unwavering loyalty were a salve to his heartstrings. With one hand he caressed her beautiful cheek. "You are his creator and therefore he will have all the protection of the Strashni, as long as he wants it." He looked up at his warrior. "Elias, teach him to fight when night falls again."

Elias nodded. He would be honored to train the savior from the Dark Prophecy.

"And, Julianna. Get some rest. Nothing more can be done in the sunshine, and you've had a very busy night." Dimas smiled at her, like a father sending his child off to bed.

She looked to the ground. "Yes, my Lord."

"And Lucas?" Dimas smiled wickedly at the unwanted guest.

Through eyes of disgust, Luke stared silently at Dimas.

"Get the fuck out of my house."

9

Theresa was up with the birds who sat outside her window, chirping. She had the sliding door open, letting in the fresh ocean air. It was a magnificent day. The sky was a pure blue with not a cloud to be seen. The air was crisp but warm from the sun. She could hear the soothing sounds of the ocean waves as she flipped the last pancake on her high-end Viking stove. She loved this life Richard allowed her to live.

Kara waltzed in, her hair up in a ponytail ready for another day of high school. Her make-up was much heavier than a fourteen-year-old should wear, but Theresa could only smile. Richard would yell at Kara for it, but Theresa loved Kara's rebellious side.

"Oooh, pancakes." Kara grabbed a pancake from

the stack on the counter.

"Hey," Theresa scolded half-heartedly. "Why don't you sit and have a plate with eggs too?"

Kara took a bite out of the pancake she was holding. "No time. Madison will be here any minute."

Theresa could see through Kara's ruse. She was sneaking off with a boy. "Well, have a great day." Theresa smiled at her youngest stepdaughter and a look passed between them. Kara knew Theresa knew. And they both said nothing.

Kara might be ready sooner than I thought, Theresa thought to herself. A honk outside alerted Kara to her ride.

"Gotta go! Bye, Theresa," Kara called over her shoulder.

Theresa finished serving Emily's and Richard's plates, setting them on the kitchen table in front of the open slider. A breeze blew in, swirling around Theresa's legs and invigorating her.

As she did every morning, she slipped love potion into Richard's orange juice.

Emily waltzed into the kitchen just as Theresa withdrew her hand from Richard's cup. Theresa smiled at her eldest stepdaughter. Emily only stared in return.

"Ready for some breakfast?" Theresa asked, a little too overly cheerful. What had Emily seen? That girl had always been a little too suspicious. Why couldn't she be more like Kara?

"Sure. Thank you," Emily responded cautiously. She wasn't smiling, but she didn't seem scared either. She sat down in front of one of the plates Theresa had set. The girl trusted her enough to eat the breakfast she'd prepared. That was a good sign.

"Good morning, darling," Richard announced, waltzing in with a kiss for Theresa. This is what she lived for. It was like they were playing house. And Theresa relished every moment of it.

"Mmmm... good morning," Theresa responded. He was dressed for the office, complete with suit and tie. He looked like a million bucks. She straightened his tie and pulled him in closer as she did so. In a soft, sultry voice she told him, "I made pancakes."

"Oh, you're a saint." He eyed the table and sat down next to his daughter. Theresa fought the urge to laugh. She'd been called many things in her four hundred years, but never a saint. "Where's Kara?"

"She got a ride from Madison," Theresa explained.

"Must have been some pipe leak. I never heard you come home last night," Richard said, his eyes on his breakfast but his voice laced with implication. She couldn't have him start questioning every little thing she did. If he started to ask too many questions, she'd have to kill him and she wasn't ready for that. Yet.

"Oh, it was. If I wasn't dealing with the damage itself, I had to take care of a ton of paperwork for the city because of it." She walked over and kissed the top of his head. Her eyes connected with Emily's, who was watching her carefully. "Don't forget to drink your orange juice. You need the vitamin C."

She smiled, still staring at Emily. Emily showed no reaction and just went back to eating her breakfast. What did she know? Or was she just suspicious?

Theresa's cell phone began ringing. She was slightly annoyed when Richard got up to see who it was.

"Elyse? There can't be more to deal with after spending the whole night at the salon." Richard looked up at Theresa.

Swallowing her frustration, Theresa declined Elyse's call. "Who knows? Elyse can be very needy. I won't worry about it today." She reached for Richard's glass of orange juice and handed it to him with a smile. She almost sighed with relief when he finally drank the juice. In an instant, his eyes were glossy and then grew wide. It was as if he could feel the potion taking over.

His shoulders slumped and the accusatory expression on his face melted away. "You shouldn't have to worry about anything. I'll always take care of you." He grabbed her and kissed her so passionately she had to lean back from the force of him.

"Gross! Really? I'm still in the room!" Emily stood up and took her plate to the sink.

Theresa and Richard giggled like busted teenagers. He helped her stand back straight and then said, "I need to get to the office anyway." In a whisper he told only Theresa, "We can pick up where we left off later."

Mission completed. The potion had had its intended affect.

When Richard was finally heading to work and Emily off to school, Theresa called Elyse back.

"We followed your instructions," Elyse explained. "He's here at the salon."

A mischievous smile danced across Theresa's lips. "Perfect. Be right there."

For the sake of pretense, she got in her car and drove away from her beach community, but she had no intention of traveling the mortal way. Once she was out of sight of nosy neighbors, she parked and headed for an alley between two stores.

One step, two, three, four...and she vanished.

Many of her witches in the Harbor Coven couldn't transport, but she'd been trained in the old magic—back when witches were taboo. Nowadays they were special, a novelty. In some ways, that annoyed her.

These weren't parlor tricks done for someone's amusement! But the cunning side of her knew this environment was more accepting of her kind, and so for that she was grateful. Hiding in plain sight made everything so much easier than when she was a young witch.

In a swirl, she re-materialized just before the red door in the back of her salon. It was early still, so there was no one in the shop. There would be no beauty appointments for another few hours. She opened the red door and strolled in to meet her coven.

They stood in a circle, chanting and dancing. Alicia, one of the older witches, was rubbing her naked body from head to toe with blood. What a celebration! Theresa beamed with joy at the sight before her.

In the center of the circle was the reason for the merriment: Marcus was on his knees, hands tied behind his back, markings on the floor beneath him to keep him powerless. His fangs were bared and he seethed, but he could do nothing but growl.

Theresa tossed her head back and laughed. All

the witches joined in, cackling with delight.

Oh, how Theresa loved toying with humans and animals, but nothing—*nothing*—compared to a good vampire-tease.

"Welcome to the Harbor Coven." Theresa spread her arms out in introduction. Marcus only snarled in return. Theresa turned her attention to Elyse, who stood at the front of the circle. "You've done well. This is Regina's right-hand man."

Elyse gloated over her prize.

"How do you know who I am? How did you know where our compound was?" Marcus spat at Theresa. If he could've moved from the center of the circle, she was positive he would've ripped her throat out.

"Ah, ah." Theresa wagged a finger at him. "I'll be asking the questions today."

"You don't know what you've done! The vampire from the Prophecy has been reborn. Now is not the time to get caught up with the Shadow Wars," Marcus growled at Theresa.

"Elyse, the mixture." Theresa held her hand out and Elyse dropped a label-less bottle into it. "I know. I've met him. He's adorable. Like a confused little kid who suddenly becomes king. I think this is exactly the right time to destroy you all." Smiling, she walked closer to Marcus, pouring some of the mixture from the bottle onto her hand and rubbing it like lotion. Marcus recoiled at the repugnant overwhelming scent of garlic. "Oh, do you like this? It's a little lotion I whipped up. Old family recipe. Crème de garlic. I think it will look lovely on your tall, dark and handsome skin."

She stepped closer, her expression that of a lion circling its wounded prey. Marcus pulled his head back, not sure what she wanted but positive it wasn't anything good.

"I want you to tell me everything about the vampire tribes fighting in the Shadow Wars. And then I want to know what you know about Shane and the Prophecy." Theresa put a garlic-lotioned hand right near Marcus' face.

Still recoiling, Marcus asked, "How do you know

so much?"

"Wrong answer." Theresa rubbed her hand across Marcus' broad shoulder, taking her time to caress his skin. He screamed in pain as his flesh sizzled from the garlic mixture. Theresa pulled her hand back. "Let's play a game. You talk, and if I don't like the answer, I burn you. Sound fun?"

"Never, you bitch!" Marcus shouted, through clenched teeth, at Theresa.

With a smile, Theresa poured more lotion in her hands and rubbed his other shoulder. Again his skin sizzled like a steak on the barbeque, leaving lumps of charred flesh where she'd rubbed.

"Okay. Shane was resurrected by his sister, a Strashni. The Prophecy says he'll one day unite all the vampires. That's all I know, I swear." Marcus panted, his shoulders smoldering.

"Unfortunately for you, I don't believe you." Theresa stepped back, reaching for a towel she was handed by one of her coven to wipe off the excess garlic lotion.

She walked over to Elyse and held out her hand again. This time Elyse handed her a small black remote. Marcus watched with suspicion, unsure of what Theresa would do.

She pressed the button and a mechanical whir began overhead. Marcus looked up.

Skylights.

The retractable coverings rolled back slowly. Only about an inch of broad daylight was coming in, but the sunlight pinpointed straight to Marcus, and he screeched in pain, his skin crackling from the burn everywhere it touched the sunlight.

"Stop!" he yelled. "I'll tell you what you want to know."

Theresa beamed. She loved torture. And it was effective. The witches giggled with glee all around her, watching and learning. "Tell me about every vampire compound. Where it is, how I get in. Leave no detail out."

"I'll tell you everything," Marcus howled, his skin still burning under the sunlight.

Theresa pushed the button and the skylight was closed again. "Oh, I know you will. Let's start with your girlfriend, Regina, shall we?"

10

Shane sat out on the patio, his face aiming up at the morning sun. He soaked in its rays, reminiscing. His bare chest warmed in the sunshine, and he let the warmth soothe him physically and emotionally. In his hand he held a photograph that represented his human life. Friends, laughter, youth.

All gone.

But he found that he wasn't angry with Julianna anymore. He wanted to be. She stole everything from him. But she also believed in him more than anyone else ever had. If he'd lived, as a human he'd probably eventually get a college degree. He'd been at a community college when his life was cut short, on the six-year plan and not caring that he was going nowhere fast. He might have gotten some dumb office job, kissing ass and making photocopies for a living. Maybe even married one day with a house, a dog and two-point-five kids. Was that the life he'd wanted?

Julianna stopped short near the sliding glass door that led to the patio, Luke right behind her. "Shane! Ohmigod get back in here!"

Shane could hear the panic in her voice, near hysteria, as if she were watching a child about to be kidnapped. He turned slowly toward his sister. "Why?"

Julianna stepped forward and her arm sizzled the moment it touched sunlight. Luke grabbed her arm and pulled her back into the house. "Can't you see? He's fine." He shook his head and leaned against the door frame. "You're just full of surprises, aren't you Shane?"

Seeing the smoke from Julianna's arm, Shane looked up to the sun. It hadn't even occurred to him that he wasn't supposed to be sitting here. Vampires can't be in sunlight. "It's not burning me at all."

"What the hell are you doing out here, Shane? We've been looking for you everywhere," Julianna scolded.

"Granted, we didn't think to check sunbathing," Luke chuckled.

Shane got up and walked over to his sister and his newfound friend. He showed them the photograph. "These were my two best friends. We'd gone beach camping last year. Surfed, fished, slept under the stars to the sounds of ocean waves..."

There was a heaviness on his face, an anchor weighing down his expression.

"I'm so sorry, Shane. I never meant to hurt you, believe it or not." Julianna's face softened and she rested a hand on his shoulder. "I know adjusting to a new life can be really hard. It wasn't that long ago for me. I remember the sense of loss when I thought about my friends and my family."

"Believe me, you'll get over it faster than you think. I don't even remember my human life much anymore," Luke added, arms folded, still leaning against the door frame.

"When were you born?" Shane asked him. He realized that Luke was one of his only friends in this new world and he knew next to nothing about him.

"1739. I came to the New World with a boatful of eager-eyed immigrants in the 1750s." Luke laughed at the memory. "What a fool I was. I thought I'd get rich in the Colonies. Instead, I became a blood-sucking monster." He shook his head. "Ah, the irony of life."

"So you were around for the American Revolution? That must've been cool to witness," Julianna added.

"Nah, by then I was long-turned and didn't give a hairy shit for human politics." His eyes grew dark. "I had plenty of my own to deal with. But I did work for Benjamin Franklin for a while. On his printing press, so that was kinda cool."

Shane shook his head. "I feel like you have quite the story to tell."

Luke flashed him his movie-star smile. "You have no idea, my newborn friend. But I'll tell you what. In all my years roaming this earth, human and vampire, I've never met a vampire who could walk in the sunlight and burn his enemies to ashes with the flick of his wrist."

Shane and Julianna exchanged a smile. Shane nodded at Luke. "You sound like you believe in me more than I believe in myself."

"Well, the Prophecy still seems like a lot of Dimas-fed horseshit, but I've seen with my own two eyes what you can do. That seems real enough to me."

Julianna put an arm around her brother. "I always knew it. I'm still blown away by it, but I always knew it. Walking in the sunlight? I mean, that's just... it's incredible."

As Julianna stood close to him, Shane noticed a bundle of clothes in her hands. "What's this?"

"I found some clothes for you. Some jeans and a T-shirt. That seemed more your style than shirtless with dress pants." Julianna held the clothes out for her brother with a warm smile. Her long blonde curls wrapped around her shoulder, and he suddenly realized how lucky he was that she was there. He'd never see his friends again from his old life. He'd never get buried in a bear hug from his mom. But he had his sister—a sister that he'd mourned five years ago—and that seemed luckier than most.

"Thanks, Jules." He took the bundle from her and she pulled him all the way inside.

"You might be able to walk in the sunlight, but I can't, and you're weirding me out," Julianna smiled. She nodded down a hallway. "Come on, let me show you which bathroom and bedroom you can use for your shower and death sleep."

Shane halted. "Death sleep? That sounds awful."

Julianna looked at Luke and they both laughed. He had so much to learn still.

Luke grabbed his shoulder. "You see, for us common vampires, there's not much to do in the daytime but hide from the sun. So we sleep and since we're dead...well, we sleep like the dead."

At the end of a hallway, Julianna indicated a room on the right. "Luke, you can stay here."

Luke hesitated. "Uh, I'm pretty sure Dimas didn't mince any words."

Julianna smiled at him, twirling a finger around a curl. "You can't go out in the daylight and, besides, you're Shane's guest. No vampire would dare defy Shane."

Luke looked up at Shane, who nodded in agreement. Where he went, Luke went. He only had so many friends in this new world.

Luke took Julianna's hand in his and kissed it dramatically. "Then until tonight, ma cherie." He entered the room backwards, closing the door behind him.

Shane just shook his head at his flirtatious friend.

Julianna was beaming when she turned around. Shane supposed Luke could be charming.

With a silly lovesick grin, she pointed to a door directly across from Luke's. "This is your room." She walked in and then pointed to an adjoining room. "That's your private bathroom."

"Julianna?" Shane sat on the end of the bed. It was perfect for him. Nondescript. Black and white.

Minimal furnishings.

"Yeah?"

"I'm sorry I yelled earlier. For blaming you." Shane stared at the floor, his picture of his best friends still there in his hand. They were happy, ocean in the background, sand and wind decorating their hair.

"Shane." Julianna squatted down in front of her brother. "Never apologize. For anything. Ever again." She grabbed his chin and forced him to look at her. "You have every right to be mad that your life was taken. And it was my fault. But for *that* I'm not sorry. I'll never be sorry. You will be the greatest vampire that ever lives. You're too important."

Shane looked straight into her eyes, the eyes that so matched his own. Even with a five-year difference in age, people had always said they looked so much alike. He'd been devastated, crushed, when she'd died. And now he had her again just like old times. Something he'd never thought was possible. "I was heartbroken when you died, Jules. Whatever this is all a part of, I can't be sorry that I woke up and saw your face first. I'm happy you're here with me."

She got up and sat next to him on the bed. "I missed you too when I resurrected. I thought about going back to get you a thousand times. And Luke is right." She pointed at the photo in his hands. "It does get easier with time."

Shane held the photo high in the air and focused on it with all his might. He'd had happy times with his friends. But they were losers on a fast-track to nowhere. And he'd been perfectly content to go nowhere with them. Was he really giving up anything so amazing? Could he actually find happiness again in this new reborn life? A corner began to smoke and then a small flame appeared, slowly making its way across the photograph. First Shane's face melted away, then each of his friends, until only ashes were left in Shane's hands.

"What are you doing?" Julianna hadn't expected him to burn something that connected him to his past.

"I didn't choose this." He shrugged. "Hell, I don't even know what *this* is. But I do know that if you and

Luke believe it, I believe it. My old life is gone. I need to focus on my new powers and learn to be who I am now."

Julianna couldn't believe what she was hearing, but the words warmed her heart like she couldn't explain. She threw her arms around Shane's neck and laughed the emotional laughter that lives somewhere between joy and being overwhelmed.

The chosen one from the Prophecy was her brother. And she'd known it all along.

It was time to get him ready for everything he was meant to do to end the Shadow Wars.

11

Dusk was making its way lazily across the Southern California sky. Regina emerged from her room, a silky robe thrown over her shoulders. She ran her fingers through her thick, black hair to smooth it out, nibbling on her lip as she did so. She was restless and couldn't hide out in her room any longer. She couldn't remember the last time she'd slept alone. Where the hell was Marcus? He hadn't come back from the battle and hadn't been counted among the dead. True that many were burnt beyond belief, but she knew him. He wasn't among the scorched either. She would send a search party to the Fortis tribe later today. If they had her precious Marcus there would be hell to pay.

And what of the scorched Bellinz? Her security

cameras had caught them simply bursting into flames—spontaneous combustion. Did the Strashni have secret witch powers, or was Shane already exhibiting some of the powers from the Prophecy?

Suddenly she regretted throwing him in her cell. It had been rash, she knew that. But rarely had anyone ever turned her down and rejection always angered her. Even before she overthrew Adolfo and became queen, male vampires had always jumped when she'd said how high. She was pretty enough, she knew that, but it had never been about looks. Men liked to conquer and she liked to manipulate. It was a perfect symbiotic relationship. And then came Shane Walker. The boy—no, the baby—from the Prophecy. What did he want if not to conquer? If not power, lust or greed?

She wasn't exactly sure how to handle someone who didn't fit the mold she knew so well.

Regina descended the stairs in a bit of a fog. Everything was different now, she knew that much. But what to do about it? She needed another chance with Shane. This time she would try being like his sister. He had seemed to respond to that. A boy with mommy issues, she supposed. She knew nothing of that either. She'd hated both her parents and murdered any soft men—human or vampire—that she'd ever met.

But Shane was both vulnerable and very powerful. A deadly combination.

She smiled to herself. Thinking of Lord Dimas's face when she stole Shane away from his clutches...ah, that just warmed the heart. She would relish doing it again.

"My queen." Alexi stood in the kitchen on the other side of the bar. The view of the ocean made a breathtaking backdrop behind him. Their compound had floor-to-ceiling windows and a small hint of orange laid upon the ocean waves as the sun set in the distance.

"Have you seen Marcus?" Regina asked.

Alexi shook his head. "Not since the battle at daybreak."

"He never came to me last night." She took a chance on showing her worry.

"I am sure he was simply celebrating his kills,

my Queen." Alexi tried to placate her, but he didn't look like he'd even convinced himself.

"We lost that battle." Her full lips were tight, squeezed so tight they were white. She took a step closer and Alexi became nervous. "Our captor was freed, many good Bellinz were killed, and Marcus is missing." She picked Alexi up by the front of his shirt and threw him back against the refrigerator with a thud. "Don't waste my time with bullshit. You will find Marcus today or find a new tribe." Her voice was soft but filled with venom. She was keeping her cool, but barely. And Alexi could see that one wrong move would cost him his life. Regina was a loving queen when she was happy, but cross her and she was unforgiving.

"Yes, Queen Regina." Alexi slowly stood up, a huge dent in the front of the fridge becoming apparent behind him. Without turning his back to her, he slid toward the front door. He only turned away from her when he got to the door because he had to. Regina watched him with a glare so dark it was like a cloud had descended inside the compound. He turned the door handle and bolted out, tripping over something underfoot on the doorstep. "My Queen?"

It was a cardboard box, like something you would ship a package in. The bottom was dark with wetness. He had no clue what it was about and he was positive he didn't want to know. His face mirrored the dread he felt straight to his core.

Silently, Regina walked toward Alexi, her face softening a little behind the curiosity. She stared at the box for a moment before instructing Alexi, "Open it."

Alexi's hands shook as he knelt back down in front of the box, extending a claw. There were few things in his life as a vampire that he'd looked forward to doing less. The foreboding he felt was like a giant boulder tied to his feet. It sank down to the ground, making him feel like he was being sucked into a sinkhole. With his long nail he slowly cut the tape at the top of the box, as if he were opening a package they had ordered via online delivery. Regina didn't rush him. She was curious but just as uncertain as Alexi. He opened one flap, then the other, then the last two.

Then Regina and Alexi both stared at the contents laying before them.

Marcus.

His head—only his head—was inside the box, eyes wide open—unseeing yet staring straight at Alexi and Regina. There were burn marks all over his cheeks. His hair on the right side was melted off, like a lava tube on his scalp. Sticky, red liquid oozed from the stump of his neck, filling Regina's nostrils with the scent of blood mixed with the acrid smell of burnt flesh.

Someone had murdered Marcus. And used him to send a message.

Regina's vision suddenly became blurry with her rage. Every wire in her brain was set off and, without control of her own movements, she began smashing everything in the foyer, screaming an inhuman howl as she did. Vase? Smashed. Pictures? Shattered. Ceramic statue? Crushed.

Vampires throughout the Bellinz compound came running out from every hallway. Some worried they were under attack again. Some were just plain curious. All went on high alert when they saw their Queen in a complete rage storm.

At the crowd, Regina stopped smashing, still breathing heavily.

It was Alexi who explained, voice shaking. "Someone has killed Marcus. We need to find the perpetrators."

"It was the Strashni who attacked yesterday. I say we pay them back," one vampire offered.

"The Strashni got what they wanted," another vampire responded.

"It was a personal vendetta. Grig of the Prudens tribe has always hated Marcus," someone else shouted.

"Enough!" Regina screamed, her voice piercing the room and echoing off every wall. Her tribe stilled before her. "I want them all dead. Anyone that does not bear the mark of the Bellinz. Kill. Them."

"We don't have the numbers for a full-on war with every tribe," Alexi said.

Regina's response was to march over to him and lift him by his throat. Her eyes were glowing as if they were on fire. "Use cunning then. Their lives or yours." She threw him out onto the front lawn. Then she turned to the vampires crowding around the foyer. "All of you. I'll kill you all if you don't get me my revenge for Marcus!"

She flew past them and up the stairs, still smashing everything she saw on her way back to her bedroom.

An unknown assailant sat watching these events. From inside the warehouse, surrounded by her coven, Theresa stared at the image playing like a movie on the bowl of water. Theresa licked her lips in delight.

Thanks for the tip, vampire betrayer. Things were working out better than planned. The vampires would soon eliminate themselves.

Now Theresa only had to figure out how to kill Shane Walker before he ended the Shadow Wars and brought peace to her most vile sworn enemy.

12

A soft rap on his door had Luke springing out of bed. His mind immediately went to Dimas, assuming the old vampire had come to kick him out of the compound. Luke rolled his eyes and opened the door with a jerk.

"Whaddya want?" he sneered. Only it wasn't the leader of the Strashni. It was Julianna, refreshed from her death sleep. Her hair was like golden silk and Luke fought the urge to touch it. She really was one of the most beautiful creatures he'd ever seen. And he'd seen his share in his lifetime.

"Are you always this cranky when you first wake up?" she smirked, rocking her shoulders seductively in front of him.

Luke stole a glance at her perfect lips and then

flashed her his debonair smile. Two can play at this game. Luke had always known his only real talent was melting women with his smolder. "I thought you were someone else. But a beautiful woman always puts the smile back on my face."

Julianna shook her head. He was over the top, but somehow it was endearing. And he was as transparent as the breeze. "You thought I was Dimas." It wasn't a question.

Luke folded his arms and leaned against the doorframe. He was still bare-chested from sleep. "Why do you trust him so much?"

Julianna matched his stance, folding her arms similarly. "Why do you not trust him at all?"

"I asked you first," Luke smiled. He had no intention of dredging up a painful past that had happened centuries ago.

Julianna watched him for a second, studying the angles of his perfect face—curious what tales he had to tell, but not wanting to push just yet. After a moment, she shrugged. "Dimas saved my life."

Luke raised an eyebrow questioningly. "And yet, here you are—dead."

She slapped his arm playfully. She enjoyed his playful banter. "My vampire life. When I was a newborn..."

"You still *are* a newborn."

"A *brand-new* newborn. I was captured by three Fortis warriors. I didn't know the hunting laws yet, and I was feeding in their territory even though I'd been branded Strashni." As if to punctuate her story, she flashed her brand mark on her forearm. Julianna shrugged again. "Dimas saved me. He slaughtered them all. It was unbelievable."

"Not really," Luke muttered. "So you've never left his side since?"

Julianna shook her head and emotion filled her eyes. "I saw the value of the tribe that day and how committed Lord Dimas was to the Strashni. I've been one of his right-hands ever since that day."

"Ah." Luke stood up straight, pushing off the wall. "Then that's the Dimas I know and love. Saving you so he could use you for his own personal slave."

"It's not like that. This tribe is everything to Lord Dimas. And me. You just don't understand the bond of a tribe." Julianna looked down at her hands for a second. Luke would never understand. How could someone with no tribe understand the devotion and ardor she felt? The tribe had a bond like family, stronger even. She would risk her life for any Strashni, let alone Dimas. And ever since that fateful day, he'd proven he would do the same for her.

Deciding there was no way she could ever convince Luke, she reached out and grabbed his hand. "Anyway, that's not why I came to you."

A hungry look passed his face. "Really?"

"I think we need to teach Shane how to hunt. He's really bad at it." Julianna giggled, thinking of that first night in the alley. She pulled Luke's hand and led him to Shane's room. "Come on."

"Let's go hunting." Julianna woke Shane up from his death sleep by running and jumping on his torso. "It's time for breakfast."

"I'm starved," Luke said, leaning up against the door frame to Shane's bedroom. "I haven't eaten anything but pig's blood in a while."

Julianna crinkled her nose. "That's disgusting."

Luke shrugged. "I've gotten used to it. That's what I'm always fed when Regina throws me in her dungeon."

"How many times have you been captured by the Bellinz?" Julianna asked.

"Three. The first time was similar to Shane's. She wanted me to be her little boy toy and I refused."

Julianna shook her head, sitting on the edge of Shane's bed as he groggily sat up. "That's awful."

"Worked out for Marcus." Luke flashed his Hollywood smile and walked over to the bedside. "So where do you guys go hunting around here?"

Julianna smiled and looked from Luke to Shane. Shane looked just as curious as Luke. "Third Street. In Santa Monica. It's a goldmine."

"I'm in." Luke took the leather jacket he'd been carrying and slipped it on. Julianna watched him carefully, staring especially at his tight shirt across his perfect abs. If this guy had a flaw, she couldn't find it.

Shane stood up and revealed his blue boxers. "Let me get dressed. Out."

Julianna stood up. "Five minutes tops. I want to go have some fun before you start uniting vampires and ending the Shadow Wars."

Julianna and Luke waited in the hallway a few minutes before Shane emerged from his bedroom dressed in jeans and a black T-shirt. He'd taken the time to smooth down the shaggy blonde hair that so often fell into his face. Julianna longed to give her brother a buzz cut, but his shaggy hair was his signature style, she supposed.

"You guys ready?" Julianna raised her eyebrows questioningly. They turned to go, and Dimas stood blocking the end of the hallway.

"Where are you three going?" Dimas asked. He tried to come off as casual, but he looked more stiff, uncomfortable.

If Julianna noticed or suspected anything, she

didn't let it show. "Going hunting in Santa Monica. Wanna come?"

Luke, however, hadn't trusted Dimas in three hundred years, so he watched a flash of darkness creep across the Strashni leader's albino-like features. It was so quick, probably no one else noticed. Or Luke had just imagined it. But he didn't think so.

The hallway was dark. No lights were on and the faint glow of dusk had long given way to moonlight. Dimas stepped from the soft glow of a patio light slipping in through the window and plunged straight into the darkness. The vampires could all see him, of course, but it somehow seemed symbolic that he should avoid any kind of light. "No. You three enjoy." He smiled. "I have other business to attend to. Shane, don't forget to begin your training."

"You don't have to remind me," Shane responded, his arms folded across his chest.

"Oh, and should you decide to join our tribe," Dimas tossed his long robe back. The effect did seem regal, "we can conduct the ceremony when you get back."

"Ceremony?" Shane asked, but he looked at Julianna.

In response, she pulled up the sleeve of her long T-shirt. "You get the mark of your tribe. It's a big honor." Shane looked at a small scar in the shape of a star. It looked like someone had taken a branding iron to his sister's arm.

"Really cosmopolitan. Branding your minions." Luke physically recoiled at the thought.

"Well," Dimas still smiled, "luckily for you no one wants you in their tribe, so you'll never have to worry about it." He bowed to the threesome, his long white hair slipping off his shoulders. "Have a fun night." And he slithered away again, presumably to his basement. His lair.

Julianna hit her brother's chest with the back of her hand playfully. "Let's go. You need to have a little fun before you start working. Be a vampire for a while before you are the one from the Prophecy."

Shane smiled in return. Everything did seem to

be happening really quickly. He barely understood what it was to be a vampire, let alone lead all the tribes. He might be ready to embrace his powers, but he wasn't ready to be their ruler. Julianna grabbed his hand and Luke followed close behind.

Santa Monica at night was bustling. The bars and shops were open and people crowded the streets. Third Street was roped off to cars so pedestrians could walk freely, stumbling around when they'd had too much to drink. Homeless people sat on every street corner asking for spare change. Street performers would do magic or play music for money in a hat or guitar case. The moon above was nearly full and already sat prominently in the sky, casting a dark blue glow to the ever-blackening night.

Julianna, Luke and Shane stood in the shadows of one of the alleys, watching the carefree people walk by.

"This time, use discretion please," Julianna instructed her brother.

"Hey. I didn't even know what was going on last

time. *Someone* hadn't explained anything to me." Shane stared back at her.

"Are we splitting up, or doing a pack-attack?" Luke asked Julianna.

"Split up. I'm not sharing," Julianna answered.

Luke lightly touched Shane's shoulder. "Come with me. I'll show you how it's done." Julianna rolled her eyes and watched as Luke and Shane stepped out of the dark alley and into the crowds of the street.

As if he'd already picked a pretty girl out of the crowd, Luke walked up to a pair of girls walking arm in arm. Shane was hard on his heels. Luke stepped in line with the girls and flashed his handsome smile at them. "Hi, ladies."

They giggled but didn't shy away from him in the slightest. Even without the benefit of vampire tricks, girls would fall at his feet simply because he was gorgeous.

"I'm Luke and this is my friend, Shane." Luke gestured at his companion. Again, the girls giggled. Shane had never been especially suave like Luke seemed to be naturally, but he flashed his best Luke-style smile. Again, they didn't back away.

"Why don't you girls come with us?" Luke asked.

They nodded in unison, their eyes glassy as if they were in a trance. He slipped his arm around the girl on the left, and nodded toward Shane to do the same to the girl on the right.

"You'll have to teach me how to do that," Shane said to Luke.

"I doubt it," Luke spoke over the girls' heads. "If you can control fire, you can control a human. It's like breathing for us vampires."

Shane pulled his girl away from Luke and the other girl. "Dance with me."

She looked puzzled, staring at him as if she had no idea where she was or what was going on. So he stared straight into her eyes and a humming sound began in his ears as the connection formed between himself and the girl in front of him. "Dance with me."

Her eyes went glassy again and she stepped closer to Shane, swaying as she did so. Luke laughed as

Shane pulled the girl close, one hand on her hip and one hand in her hand. They did a crappy rendition of a waltz and after a few back-and-forths, he spun her around with one hand. It was contrived, but the girl seemed to be having a good time. She was smiling.

"It's time," Luke whispered to Shane. "Go up against the wall of that store and pretend you are kissing her neck."

"Right here in front of everyone on the street?" Shane asked, the girl still trying to dance with him.

"Oh, that's the best way. Hiding in plain sight." Luke smiled. "Told you we were monsters. But a growing boy has to eat." Then he quickly added, "Humans only see what they want to see anyway."

Shane looked down at the pretty girl still dancing around his feet, and he grabbed her again, pulling her close, and kept dancing while Luke took his girl over to the wall. Shane watched Luke slide his lips down her jawline to her neck. He knew the moment Luke had pierced skin as the girl's eyes widened, and then went slack.

Shane stopped the girl he was dancing with, holding both her arms at her side. "Listen to me." The humming began again and he stared deep into her eyes. "Your friend is really drunk. You need to go home and lock your doors. It's not safe for you out here."

She nodded like a small child being given instructions, and then she ran off. He might be a monster, but he wasn't going to cut short another young life just as his own had been. And part of him thought, maybe if he drank some and stopped, she might live But, truth be told, he wasn't sure he could stop.

So he changed tactics.

Standing in the middle of the street, he closed his eyes, letting his hearing take over his senses. Down the street a ways, he heard a woman yelling. Then a man's voice, speaking sternly. They were arguing. *That might work*, he told himself.

He walked purposefully in the direction of the scuffle. He got closer and saw a woman shoved into a small patio table that was set up in front of a restaurant. The glasses and plates that had been on the table were knocked to the ground, exploding in fragments at her feet. A large man with a long beard stood over her, fuming. Shane approached just as the man pulled his hand up and across his chest to backhand the cowering woman, even as other patrons watched and did nothing.

Shane grabbed the man's raised hand and squeezed.

"What's going on here?" he asked, as casually as he could muster.

The bearded man tried to yank his hand out of Shane's grip. He was unsuccessful. "Nothing that concerns a little punk like you."

Shane looked over at the woman, who was trying to stand up from where she'd fallen against the table. Mascara was running down her face.

"Are you okay?" Shane asked her. She nodded. "Get out of here." She ran, stumbling and limping as she left. Shane turned toward Beardie. "Let's go somewhere and talk, shall we?"

"Fuck you." Beardie hocked a chunk of something from the back of his throat and spit it with full force onto Shane's face. Shane was shocked, but barely. He casually wiped the wad of spit from the left side of his nose, tossing it on the ground with a splat. Beardie laughed, his hand still squeezed like a vise in Shane's grip.

Yep. He'd chosen his prey wisely. This guy was human garbage.

Calmly and without saying a word, Shane let go of Beardie's hand and grabbed the front of his shirt, throwing him onto a table. It shattered beneath the large man. Onlookers gasped and backed away, trying to avoid getting sucked into the bar brawl.

It was amazing what people would ignore. *Humans see what they want to see.*

Shane walked over to Beardie slowly, like a lion calculating his pounce on his prey. Beardie, surprised by Shane's superhuman strength, backed away from the oncoming predator. He was finally realizing this wasn't going to end well for him. No matter. Shane caught up to him easily and grabbed his right foot.

"So you like to beat up women, huh?" Shane

asked as he pulled Beardie's leg, dragging him along behind himself like a rag doll. Tables, chairs, pedestrians were all banged and bumped as he trod along. People gasped but did nothing—just as they'd done nothing to help the woman Beardie had been roughing up. Shane dragged him behind the buildings and stood behind a dumpster so no one would see what he was about to do. If he needed to kill to stay alive, he could at least select victims that were dregs on society. Do the world a favor.

The last thing Beardie saw was Shane's fangs extend two inches from his face. He started to yell for help, but his scream was cut off as Shane pierced his neck and began to drain him. Perhaps he'd made the hole in Beardie's neck a little too huge. Blood still poured all down Shane's neck and onto the front of his black shirt. So he still hadn't mastered that skill. He was going to be a bloody mess again.

In less than a minute, the large, bearded bully was a lifeless meat suit. Shane could actually feel his life force drain with his blood. He knew the instant he was gone. A tiny drop of guilt swirled with the supreme sense of satisfaction he felt at that precise moment.

With one hand, he picked Beardie up and debated throwing him in the dumpster. He decided it was probably better not to leave any unanswered questions behind. Concentrating on his hands, he pushed fire through his fingertips, watching the flames but not feeling the heat as Beardie's limp body burnt to tiny ashes at his feet. A breeze came by and picked up several of the chunks of ash. Shane watched as the remnants of what was once Beardie was carried away toward the Pacific Ocean. He wondered for a brief moment if anyone would miss that bully but then swallowed down the thought as quickly as it had entered his mind. There was one less monster in the world, and Shane would be all right with that.

"I told you, Luke." Julianna came around the corner toward Shane. "That burning smell was Shane."

"Hey guys." Shane nodded at Julianna and Luke. "You done?"

"Holy shit, Shane. What did I tell you about

discretion? You are the messiest eater." Julianna began wiping up his neck and chin with the sleeve of her shirt.

"And the scene at the bar back there looks like a war zone," Luke added. "What happened to the girl I gave you?"

"If I have to be a monster, I'm going to attack the monster bigger than me," Shane said calmly.

Luke smiled. "I like it. Vigilante vampire. Burning their remains is a nice touch too."

Shane shrugged. "It was a spur of the moment decision."

"Look, boys. As much as I'd love to stand around by the dumpster talking about who we ate for dinner and why, we gotta get back to the compound. Dimas called me. Marcus has been killed and Regina is on a rampage."

"Marcus is dead?" Shane asked, truly shocked.

Luke just added, "Serves them both right."

"You don't have to feel sorry for Marcus, but this is going to ramp up the violence between tribes. Shane's rebirth is supposed to be bringing it to an end." Julianna chewed her lip, worry written all over her face.

Luke grabbed her hand and kissed it gently, and then he rubbed her arm to soothe her. He was such a flirt. "Shane barely knows how to eat. He's not ready to be a savior yet."

"I'm right here, guys, and I have superhuman hearing," Shane said, rolling his eyes.

Julianna didn't take her eyes off Luke's. She smiled coyly as he continued rubbing her arm far longer than was necessary. Shane cleared his throat.

Reluctantly, Julianna turned her gaze from Luke to Shane. "Lord Dimas will have a plan. Let's just get back and talk to him."

"You keep saying Dimas has all the answers, but so far I'm not seeing it," Shane answered.

Julianna touched her brother's arm. "Give him a chance. You'll see how truly brilliant he is."

Shane looked over at Luke, remembering the animosity. "What happened between the two of you?"

"It was a long time ago," Luke shrugged.

"Should I trust him?" Shane asked Luke directly.

Luke looked uncomfortably at Julianna. It was clear that on the issue of Lord Dimas they were a divided front. "I don't." Luke looked at the ground, watching a piece of ash float lazily on a breeze at Shane's feet. "You can come to your own conclusions."

"Fine. Let's go talk to Dimas." Shane stood up straight. "But I'm not Strashni and I'm not his pawn. If I don't like what he has to say, I'll make my own plan."

"You'll come to see he is a good ruler and could be a great mentor for you, Shane. Trust me." Julianna implored her brother with her eyes, wide and soft.

Shane nodded. "I'll give him a chance."

"If it doesn't work with Lord Dumbass, you can always join my merry band. The tribeless wanderer always has room," Luke smirked at Shane.

Julianna laughed but then saw her brother's face. He was actually tempted to run around tribeless with Luke. "No. That is not an option for the chosen vampire. He is an elite member of the ruling class, not some nomad outcast."

Luke winced at her words, but he recovered

quickly. "I'm just saying, sometimes your judgment is less cloudy when you're not caught up emotionally."

Julianna swallowed hard but said nothing. Shane sensed the tension but couldn't completely side with either of them. He respected both their opinions and also felt they both had valid points. And also, he didn't really care about vampire politics and Shadow Wars. They meant nothing to him.

But he also knew he didn't owe anybody anything. If he was going to be some great savior, it was going to be on his own terms.

Stepping between them, he said again, "I'll listen to Dimas with an open mind and come to my own conclusions."

13

The Fortis compound was an old hunting lodge high up in the mountains. The moon was high in the sky casting a glow on the tops of the trees, with shadows of branches littering the ground. At the top of the mountain, inside the lodge, there was a party going on. The music echoed through the forest-covered mountain top, the sound of the bass thump-thumping against the surrounding tree trunks.

Damian, their tribe leader, sat sideways in a reclining armchair, his feet dangling over the armrest. Even though the snow had long since melted in the Southern California sun, he wore his snow boots with jeans. His red and black flannel shirt was unbuttoned, revealing his muscular chest. He winked at Ignacio, who was playing DJ. Notch, as they all called him, was good with music—always had been.

Dahlia danced in a skimpy dress in front of Damian, no doubt trying to get his attention. She had no sense of rhythm. Whatever song was playing in her head, it wasn't the one Notch was spinning. Her hips swayed slowly as the beat pounded quickly. Damian just shook his head at how ridiculous she looked. Two Fortis women were dancing seductively in the corner where they'd found a tiny pocket of shadow. Almost every surface had someone dancing on it—counters, tables, chairs, the floor. Humans lay scattered about the main room of the lodge, leftover feeders from earlier feasting, still dazed and drunk from their sacrifice to the Fortis tribe.

This is a good party, Damian thought to himself.

Damian leaned way back, his head resting on the arm of the chair, staring up at the high ceilings and exposed beams above him. He'd ripped the animal heads off the walls decades ago, but this place was still so rustic to him. One day he'd need to focus on interior decorating and make this place a little more modern.

"What are we doing about the Prophecy?" Isabelle asked, shouting over the sound of the music, her cold hard stare digging deep into Damian's eyes. She sat on the hearth in front of a raging fire that twisted, turned and popped in the background.

Damian rolled his eyes at her. "You take things too seriously. Just enjoy yourself for once, Isabelle. This is a party."

"And you don't take things seriously enough, Damian," Isabelle snapped. She was pretty, but tough. The first thing people noticed when they saw her was her stern expression. If she rode off on a motorcycle with a machine gun on her back, no one would think twice. But if they stared long enough, they might see smooth olive skin, long pretty brown hair, high cheek bones.

Damian was once very fond of Isabelle. She balanced him out, and there had been a time when he would seek her out for her advice. Now she was ruining his party with the giant stick up her ass and it was getting on his nerves. He was tiring of his Number Two, but he was well aware that many Fortis vampires would choose her over him. So he tolerated her.

"Isabelle. We're immortal. Enjoy the many tomorrows you are presented with. Go find someone to play with your boobs and leave me to enjoy my party." Damian stood up and sauntered over to Notch, placing an arm over his shoulders seductively and whispering something in Notch's ear. Whatever he said made Notch smile shyly.

"Ancient ignorant bastard," Isabelle muttered under her breath. Dahlia moved her terrible dancing a step closer to where Isabelle sat. "Get out of my face."

But instead of obeying, Dahlia, still moving and twisting her hips to some unheard beat, reached out for Isabelle. Isabelle stood, no smile on her face, and shoved Dahlia backward. Dahlia flew, crashing across the room into an end table with a lamp. The table and the lamp smashed to the floor. Notch and Damian watched and laughed at the sight. The music never stopped and most vampires didn't even notice—they kept dancing.

Dahlia stood up and brushed herself off. If she was mad, she didn't show it. She just started dancing again. Fortis vampires were used to Isabelle.

Isabelle had chosen the Fortis because they were once the toughest warriors. She had bet her life that they would win the Shadow Wars. Now she wasn't so sure. Under Damian's leadership, they hid high up in the mountains partying while the Dark Prophecy played out with the Strashni and Bellinz. She wasn't sure how much more she could take. The time for action was upon them, and her tribe had chosen to bury their heads in the sand and act like impudent children.

She wanted to scream and hit something.

She stared at the mark on her forearm, the tattoo in the shape of a flame that symbolized the Fortis tribe. It was becoming a mark of shame. Extending a claw on her index finger, she began to pick at the mark slowly, scratching it until she bled. A drop of blood trickled down her arm, and she watched it slowly drip to the stone hearth beneath her. If she had to, she would lead a team on her own to go find the one they were all speaking about, the young vampire who had resurrected in St. Mary's Cemetery.

She had to do something. She couldn't just relax and party like Damian. It wasn't in her nature. She stood to go find the team she trusted the most, to organize the search party. But she'd barely taken a step when the window by the front door of the large cabin shattered, crashing glass and window frame all around the front of the main hall.

The music instantly stopped and every Fortis vampire turned, senses on high alert.

Easily forty Bellinz vampires came trouncing through the broken window and gathering in front of where the Fortis had been partying moments ago. Alexi was in the lead.

"Who killed Marcus?" he shouted, his voice bellowing through the large expansive room. Behind him, every Bellinz vampire seethed, fangs and claws extended.

It was Isabelle who stepped forward. Finally, this party was getting good. And she knew she had to be the one to act. Damian still huddled by Notch in the shadows. "Get the fuck out of here. And take your Bellinz babies with you."

Alexi removed his gloves slowly, something he'd watched Marcus do plenty of times. In fact, he was dressed nicely in a long black leather coat just as he'd seen Marcus do in the past. "What's the party for, Isabelle? What are you celebrating?"

"None of your fucking business, Alexi." Isabelle stepped forward. She could feel her blood getting hotter under her skin and it excited her. She knew she was moments away from ripping flesh off bones. "Get out of my compound." Secretly she hoped he didn't listen so she could have the fight she was itching for.

Alexi didn't back away. "Regina wants answers." He stepped casually toward Isabelle. Then he paused and smiled, his fangs glistening in the firelight. "Actually, she wants you all dead, but I'm giving you a chance to explain why you killed Marcus."

"Why would we kill Marcus?" Damian shouted from the shadows where he still remained hidden.

Isabelle groaned at his weakness.

"All I know is Marcus is dead, Regina is rightfully upset, and you all are up here celebrating." He stared at Isabelle again. "Looks suspicious."

Isabelle stepped forward herself, putting her face inches from Alexi's. She extended her own fangs to show she wasn't afraid. "You think I give a shit what you think?"

Her words hung in the air for a moment and silence filled the room, all eyes on Isabelle and Alexi and the standoff between them. The truth was Isabelle wished she *had* killed Marcus. The Fortis tribe hadn't done one offensive thing in the Shadow Wars in ages. But they'd been partying while Marcus was killed, and she wouldn't allow the fruity little Bellinz babies to come in here and accuse her of anything in her own home.

It was only a slight nod, but Isabelle noticed the signal when Alexi gave it.

She grabbed for his throat, claws extended, only half a second before he grabbed her shoulders and threw her. Her grip wasn't strong enough on him and she was hurled back toward the fireplace.

And then the Bellinz vampires attacked.

The Fortis were ill-prepared for battle. They'd been dancing, drinking, enjoying their hedonism. Dahlia was ripped to pieces, literally arms and legs pulled apart from her trunk, before Isabelle had even gotten back up. She might have been the world's worst dancer, but Isabelle seethed at the offense. No one comes in here and kills her fellow Fortis tribe members on her watch.

From her peripheral vision, Isabelle watched Damian sneak into the shadows. How fitting. *Once a coward always a coward.* And then she pounced on Alexi, knocking him backward. She landed on his chest, her fangs inches from his face, spit dripping from her mouth. Before she could bite his face off, he shoved her to the left and she rolled off Alexi and onto the floor. He was quickly back up to his feet and so she kicked straight to the groin with her heel, a wicked smile upon her lips. He doubled over and she stood up laughing.

Every part of her body was zinging. The smell of blood all around her was intoxicating and the thrill of the battle was energizing.

At long last, something was happening around here. Isabelle rolled her shoulders, taking in the moment she relished.

She slowly walked behind Alexi and pulled his hair, yanking his head backward. She extended her claws on her free hand to slice his throat. And then a force knocked her to the ground again, pain searing her arm. A blonde female Bellinz stood above her panting. She looked to Isabelle like easy prey.

Fighting two at once? Twice the exhilaration. Bring it.

Isabelle swept her leg beneath the Bellinz vampire, taking her legs out from underneath her. As the Bellinz woman fell, Isabelle caught her and threw her at Alexi. Alexi and the blonde both stumbled backward toward the fire.

Battle raged all around the compound. Bodies and limbs went flying, blood was splattered. The Fortis might have been jumped, but they weren't going down easily, Isabelle noticed. They would lose a few, but the prissy Bellinz were shitty fighters so she knew they'd lose a few too.

She ran at Alexi and the woman. Alexi would be a battle, but the woman she just wanted dead. So she yanked Alexi's foot and threw him behind her toward the front door and the glass of the broken front window. The blonde began to scamper away, but Isabelle wagged a finger at her. And then she pounced.

Pinning the blonde with her arms and legs, Isabelle bit at the woman's neck. Sure, she could have just ripped her head off, but Isabelle wanted the taste of blood. So, she bit the front of her throat, pulling off the flesh. Then she did the same to the back, biting off most of her neck, until there was barely a spinal cord holding the head to the body. And then Isabelle bit through that too, and the blonde woman's head rolled off the hearth, landing on the floor with a plunk.

She stood, smiling, eyes laser-focused on Alexi. She wiped her mouth with the back of her hand, smearing blood across her face. Right next to her, a Fortis vampire—Trenton, one of her favorites—bit the arm off a Bellinz warrior. She stepped over the stump of his arm and toward Alexi. Alexi stood to face Isabelle, no sign of fear and clearly recovered from the earlier sucker kick.

Good. This will be more fun.

She yelled as she ran toward him with full force. Preparing for her attack, he crouched and spread his legs in a power stance. He extended his arm and caught her before she could jump on him, lifting her upward with one hand. She easily knocked his arm away and landed gently at his feet.

She kicked. He blocked. He punched. She dodged.

She climbed on his back to choke him from behind, but he yanked her over his head, and she somersaulted at his feet, pulling him with her into a roll. She landed on top of him and he shoved her off. She flew back from the force, but not nearly as much as earlier since now she was expecting it. She slid a few feet and then ran back toward him, arms extended and claws out. Isabelle dug her nails into his shoulders, extending her claws as far as they could go, piercing through his flesh as she did so. He winced, but ever so slightly before he hit her square in the nose. Her face crunched as blood splattered and she let go of Alexi to reel from the blow. Her ears were ringing as she cracked her nose back into place, smiling with excitement.

Alexi grabbed Isabelle's arm to throw her again, but someone stood in his way.

"Stop!" that someone shouted. Alexi turned to see Shane Walker, with Luke, Elias and Julianna at his side.

Isabelle and Alexi stopped fighting, mostly because they were curious what was going on, but no other vampires did. The room was still packed with the sounds and sights of fangs, flesh and flying body parts.

Shane watched for a moment as Alexi and Isabelle watched him, taking in the scene before him.

Isabelle became annoyed at yet another intruder in her compound. "What the hell do you want?"

Shane looked at her but didn't answer. Instead, he concentrated on the fire burning violently in the fireplace. He was faster with his powers now, and he easily sucked the fire into the air in the center of the room, creating a spinning ball of fire that floated above them all. "Stop or I'll burn you all with a flick of my wrist."

The Bellinz vampires, having already seen the results of his firepower, instantly stopped fighting and backed away from their opponents. The Fortis vampires stopped too because they had no idea what their eyes were seeing. Whispers began passing from vampire to vampire. Was this the one from the Dark Prophecy?

He might have been showing off a little, but he was also trying to subdue them with awe in his abilities. Maybe to get them to believe in the Prophecy? Shane moved his hands around and, in concert with his movements, the ball of fire took various shapes. A dragon. A sword. A dodecahedron.

Isabelle watched, barely trusting her own eyes.

"How are you doing that?"

Eyes glued to the morphing fire-shapes, Alexi responded with his voice filled with wonder, "He's the one from the Prophecy."

No one argued and Shane neither confirmed nor denied. He simply stepped into the center of the room, Julianna, Luke and Elias at his side, just as always. He continued to play with the fire as he spoke. "What is going on here?"

It was Notch who shouted out from the shadows, "The Bellinz tribe accused us of killing Regina's partner, Marcus. They attacked us unprovoked."

Shane looked at Alexi with a raised brow.

Alexi nodded. "Regina ordered us to kill them all in revenge for Marcus' death."

As if in response to Alexi's words, Theresa's face popped into his mind's eye. He didn't know how he knew—was this a new power?—but he *knew* she was somehow behind all this. When they'd gotten back from hunting, Lord Dimas had told them what he knew: that

Regina was on a killing spree out of spite for Marcus's death. But he'd had no other details. In fact, he'd strongly encouraged Shane to let them fight it out as they always did.

"It wasn't vampires who killed Marcus," Shane announced, his voice powerful with confidence. He wasn't especially muscular, or tall, but somehow he commanded the room with his presence. Whispers began again, everyone wondering what he could possibly be talking about. "It was the witches. I don't know what they're after, but I have no doubt that you all killing each other plays right into their hands."

Isabelle could sense Shane's power and it both thrilled and frightened her. As she always had done, she acted on impulse. She quickly grabbed the leg of a broken end table that lay on the floor at her feet and stuck it in the fireball raging in the air above Shane's head. "There's no way you could know that." She waved her torch in Shane's and Luke's faces. Julianna instantly stood in front of her brother to protect him. "Why should we trust you?" Isabelle added. "A Strashni invading my home with far too much knowledge about witches?"

Shane stepped around Julianna and came inches from Isabelle's flame. Fire had long since stopped hurting him. He felt no heat at all, despite it dancing across his flesh. "I'm not Strashni." He looked back at Luke. "I'm tribeless."

Gasps and whispers erupted again, spreading around the room.

Just as he had with other powers he'd discovered accidentally, he suddenly felt in his gut that he could call to water. He felt it nearby—a lake or river perhaps? He closed his eyes and called to it. A giant water droplet came flying in the broken window and he used it to douse Isabelle's torch, drenching her in the process.

"I believe in one united tribe of vampires," he said to the whole room. "Stop this senseless fighting. And Bellinz tribe—go home." As punctuation to his sentence, he sent the fireball back to the fireplace.

"The water's new." Luke leaned into Shane.

Julianna smiled. "He's getting more powerful."

A dripping wet Isabelle dropped to one knee, in awe of this new vampire. Finally, someone powerful. A stirring in her soul told her that the life she craved was allied to him. She felt no remorse about leaving the Fortis compound with this boy from the Prophecy. Damian be damned. "My Lord. I'll serve you always."

"Great," Shane reached out a hand and helped the pretty brunette to stand. "You can come with me and help Elias teach me to fight."

14

"Again!" Isabelle shouted and Shane ran at her full force. She smiled with glee as he tackled her.

"I think she's getting her jollies." Elias took a swig of blood from his canteen. He sat in the corner watching, having already spent most of the early evening teaching Shane proper form for throwing a punch or kick.

From underneath Shane, Isabelle pushed him off her and he flew against the wall. She stood, glowering. "Don't be afraid to use your weight. Or your claws. Extend them."

Shane did as she instructed and his claws grew three inches past his fingertips. And then he ran at Isabelle again, full force, claws extended. And calmly, Isabelle lifted her leg, colliding with Shane's stomach, sending him backward. Again.

"And don't be so predictable," she smiled at him.

Trying to be creative, he stood across from Isabelle, squaring up his shoulders. He threw a punch, but he added a fireball to his fist as it connected with her jaw. It scorched her face as she flew backward. "You said to be unpredictable."

Elias laughed in the corner.

Isabelle touched her blackened cheek and winced from the burn. "Yeah. I did. And you should use whatever you have to your advantage. That's good." She came back to Shane. "I wish I could throw a fire-punch. I'd be a total badass."

"You're a badass anyway," Shane answered. She was surprised to see he wasn't kidding. No one had ever respected her skills before. Damian had always thought her too intense and barely tolerated her anymore. "Now show me how you ripped off all those limbs last night."

She smiled—a genuine smile. "That's easy. The trick is twisting as you pull. Pulling hard enough works too, but it's harder. If you twist as you pull," she demonstrated with his wrist, just not using force, "you lessen the resistance and it pops off twice as fast."

Elias stood, coming back to join them in the center of the home-based gym inside the Strashni compound. "You are a bloodthirsty woman, Isabelle."

Isabelle shrugged. She'd been called worse, and she also knew she couldn't deny it. She loved fighting and killing. She wouldn't apologize for it. "We all have our talents."

"Spar with me," Elias smiled at her. She took the bait and got into a crouched fighting stance. She smiled back. It was an honor to teach Shane, but he was just a beginner. Elias would actually be a challenge. And his expression told her that he thought the same about her.

"And I'll go take a shower." Shane announced his departure just as Elias swiped at her legs. He was going easy on her and Shane knew that meant one thing: he would lose. Shane suspected many a vampire had ended in pain by underestimating Isabelle. As he left the room, Shane heard her laughing at Elias.

Heading up the dark stairwell toward his

bedroom, Shane wondered how much he cared about what a terrible fighter he was. If he could burn his opponent to a crisp in one second flat, did he need to know how to throw a punch? Perhaps not, but he didn't want to have to rely on superpowers. There was always a point where good old fashioned hand-to-hand combat came into play and he wanted to be prepared. And in the mountains, he discovered he could call to water just as he did with fire. That could come in handy.

But how was any of this going to stop the Shadow Wars? He had no idea.

He'd only been a vampire for less than a week, and already he felt the burden of leading them all.

The hall near his bedroom was dark, but he could see fine. In fact, he was finding that he enjoyed the darkness. It was somehow soothing to his vampire soul. But his ears were sensitive now too, and there was a sound in the hallway. It wasn't normal.

He paused at the end of the hall, hesitating to move and scare away whatever or whoever was there.

A scuffling noise came scratching through.

It was just up ahead. Shane walked slowly, foot over foot. Could some vampire from another tribe be here to grab him again? Or could it be witches? If they beheaded Marcus, what kind of prize might Shane be?

Stepping lightly again he extended his claws, preparing to fight as Isabelle had taught him. *Don't be predictable.*

And there was the sound again, growing a bit louder. It was coming from the hall closet. Someone was definitely in there.

Creeping up to it, Shane steeled himself for the fight.

He squared off in front of the closet, hesitating with his hand an inch from the door handle, claws extended. Suddenly the door thudded, a physical bump forcing it to rattle in its door jamb.

And then...a giggle? What the hell?

With a look of part confusion and part frustration, Shane opened the door quickly. Nothing could prepare him for what he saw.

"Get out!" Shane shouted at a half-naked Luke,

whose body was pressed against his sister's.

Luke instantly put his hands up, exposing Julianna's breasts. She only laughed. "This isn't what it looks like, Shane."

Luke went to zip up his pants and Shane grabbed his arm and threw him out of the closet, slamming Luke's body against the wall behind him. "I think it's exactly what it looks like, Luke," Shane growled. Turning to Julianna, he ordered, "Get dressed."

Ignoring her brother, a totally naked Julianna leaned against the closet door frame watching the scene unfold. Shane turned around to pick Luke up again.

As he stepped toward Luke, Luke said, "It's different than the other girls I told you about, Shane. I love Julianna."

Shane hesitated for a split-second before grabbing Luke's arm. "Wrong answer." And he threw Luke down the hall toward their bedrooms. Luke stood up, knowing it was useless to fight back. He stood there, eyes pleading with Shane, but said nothing.

Sensing that her brother might take things too

far, Julianna came up behind Shane. "Settle down, Shane. You've been a vampire for two seconds. You don't have to be such a prude."

Shane turned to her. "I don't want him touching you." He averted his eyes and then shielded them with his hand. "I can't even look at you."

This made Julianna laugh again. "Shane. You're not my dad. You're not even my tribe leader. This is none of your business."

"You're my sister and Luke's my best friend. Do you know what a bad sitcom this sounds like?" Shane snarled.

Luke stepped forward. "Best friend?"

Snapping his head toward Luke, Shane answered, "Ex-best friend."

Julianna shoved her brother and then sauntered toward her bedroom, making no move to hide any part of her naked body from anyone who might enter the hallway. "We need to get you a girlfriend, Shane." And then she closed the door behind her.

"It really is different, Shane. Your sister is unlike

anyone I've ever met in hundreds of years," Luke whispered.

"Stop saying that," Shane said, walking past Luke and toward his own bedroom, "or I will kill you."

Shane closed the door, leaving Luke standing in the middle of the hallway where two Walkers he cared about had both slammed the door and left him. What was it about that family? He'd never cared about anyone in hundreds of years. And now he found that he'd lay his life down for either of them.

Bastards.

15

Theresa walked into her salon to see the betrayer of the vampires standing right in front of the red door to her warehouse.

"What do you want? Our business is through," Theresa demanded.

"Nicely done with Marcus. I always hated that man-whore." His long hair fell into his face.

"Then you'll be happy to know he cried like a baby at the end." Theresa leaned on one leg and folded her arms. "Now what do you want? If you just wanted to send me a compliment, you could have emailed me."

The betrayer smiled, his fangs elongated. "I have information for you that you might find useful."

"I want nothing from you." Theresa pushed past him and reached out for the red door.

"There is a tribe of vampires leaving town, trying to sneak away," he whispered wickedly. "You could slaughter a whole tribe in one shot."

She froze with her hand on the knob. "And why would I want to kill a tribe of vampires?" Even though she did. She turned back to the betrayer. "And more importantly, why do you?"

He was close. Too close. He smelled like decaying flesh and dried blood. His skin was so pale it was almost translucent. Like all vampires, his very existence disgusted her. "I have my reasons, as do you. You know as well as I do that there are benefits to us working together."

"Show me your mark," Theresa instructed. She didn't trust this vampire even as he tempted her.

He pulled his sleeve down, revealing nothing. "Just know it works for both of us if you kill the Prudens."

Theresa took in a long breath. So he likely wasn't Prudens. Then again, maybe it was his tribe. He'd already proven he had no qualms about backstabbing. "Tell me what you know, and I'll *think* about murdering them. And only if it benefits *me*."

He smiled, his fangs still extended. She smiled back leaning into him, not even an ounce of fear of his fangs in her face. Two could play at this game. She knew he was using her, but what was his end game? And what was hers?

She did want the vampires all destroyed, mostly because she hated them. But also they got in the way an awful lot with their silly turf wars. The world would be a better place without them in it. Magic was natural, so witches were an extension of nature. These monsters were an affront to nature. They were wrong in every way. If she started down this path, she'd have to see it through, even eventually killing the betrayer himself. He had to know that.

But for now they needed each other so both would stay alive at the moment. Then one day, they would be trying to kill each other. Theresa just had to make sure she struck first.

"They are at the California-Oregon border.

Hiding out in the Cascade-Siskiyou National Forest. You can't miss them. A large group of blood-suckers killing humans can't hide out for long."

He turned to go, his long jacket fanning out behind him.

"What's in this for you?" Theresa asked. She could take some guesses, but she really wanted to hear him say it.

Without turning around he answered, "Everything. The very Prophecy is at stake." And he snuck out into the shadows.

Theresa leaned against the red door, deciding if she wanted to kill the Prudens. Did it matter what this vampire's reasons were? She would kill him the next time she could. She knew the potion they'd given him wouldn't do much to protect him. She'd made sure of it. And two could play at that game anyway. Wouldn't be the first time someone tried to kill her.

So why was she thinking of Shane Walker?

The betrayer said the Prophecy was at stake. But the Prudens looked like they were fleeing. Surely they hadn't tried to kill or kidnap Shane? And if they had, what trap might she be walking into?

Damn. She couldn't trust that betraying vampire. But still she had to hedge her bets.

She pulled her cell phone from her pocket, dialing Elyse. She trusted Elyse more than she trusted anyone or anything in this world. The bond of witches in a coven was naturally strong, but Elyse was like a sister to her on top of it all. After two rings, Elyse answered. "Elyse. I have new information. There's a tribe of vampires up near the California-Oregon border. Take a team with you and kill as many as you can."

"As you wish," Elyse responded, no hesitation in her voice. She would drink poison for Theresa. "And what will you be doing?"

"I'm going to pay a little visit to the baby vamp from the Prophecy. I want to make sure he's still alive," Theresa responded. "Let me know when your deed is done."

"Will do." Elyse hung up and Theresa stared at the phone in her hand.

Finding Shane would be easy. She'd taken hairs from the scene when she'd found him in the Bellinz basement. Granted they were Julianna's hairs, but she knew the two were never too far from one another willingly. Using Julianna's hair, she quickly whipped up a locator spell in the warehouse behind her salon, adding ingredients and stirring, dropping in Julianna's hair as the final reaction took place and the potion began to bubble and smoke. She was just about to drink it when her phone rang again.

Richard. *Shit.*

"Hi, honey." She poured it on thick, trying to sound amorous. Living this double life had always been easy, but now it was starting to become a chore. She might have to get rid of Richard sooner than she'd planned. That bummed her out.

"Are you okay? You're usually home by now." Richard's voice was laced with concern, and that warmed her heart. He was truly worried about her.

"I'm absolutely fine, honey. Just finishing payroll. It took me a bit longer than I expected this week. I'll be home in a few." She lowered her voice, trying to sound seductive. "Wait for me, will you?"

"Of course, T. I've just been so worried about you. The girls are worried. We love you." He sounded so sincere. And Theresa loved being needed. So maybe she wouldn't be killing him just yet.

"And I love you too. Wrapping up soon and I'll see you in a bit. Kiss those girls for me." She hung up and made a gagging face. One stepdaughter was a bitch and the other was a heartbeat away from being a felon. Oh, the prices we pay!

She tossed her head back and drank the potion. A small wave of dizziness and then she found herself standing in a bedroom. The shower was on and someone was singing. A girl's voice. Julianna. Theresa pulled the black hood of her cape up over her face and opened the bedroom door. She stepped into a dark hallway with many doors all along it. Any one of these could be Shane's door, and she really didn't relish the thought of running into other random vampires.

But she knew he wouldn't be far from Julianna,

so with confidence she opened the door directly across from Julianna's room.

Shane sprang from his bed, where he'd been lying and pouting. Surprise at his guest was clearly written on his face.

"Sulking doesn't become you," Theresa announced as she pulled her hood down, revealing her dark brown hair cascading across her shoulders.

She watched him transition from shock to steely resolve. He stood up straight, chest out, chin held high. If this was just bravado, she had to give him credit. He looked much more regal than when she'd first met him.

"How'd you find me?" Shane asked through piercing eyes.

Theresa walked over to his dresser and inspected the items upon it. A brush. A wallet. Some after-shave. "A witch has her ways. I don't mean to brag, but we're very powerful."

He watched her carefully. She touched nothing but scrutinized everything. "I believe you. And I assume you came back to see what I thought about your offer?"

Theresa smiled. She liked this kid. Under different circumstances, she might have considered making him a warlock in her Harbor Coven. "Your betrayer visited me again today. I don't like his games."

"Then why play them?"

Theresa looked up. He was shrewd. Rather than connect with him over this betrayer, she was pushing him away. Time to change tactics. "I think he may want your job as uniter of all vampires. I could help you if he tried to make a move against you."

Shane stepped forward, carefully, methodically. But also menacingly. His eyes darkened. "Ah, but can I trust *you*? You killed Marcus, trying to incite more infighting."

Theresa shrugged, as if the death of vampires was a price that had to be paid. "I needed information. You must understand that I have a coven to protect. They look to me just as the vampires all look to you." She tried her best to look vulnerable, batting her eyes and tightening her lips. "It can be quite the burden."

A look flashed in his eyes, and Theresa knew

she'd struck a chord. But he hid it quickly. "You didn't have to kill him."

"I do what needs to be done."

"As do I." Shane took another step forward, his fangs elongating. She looked at his hands. No claws. Was he just trying to scare her? She was a powerful witch and trusted she could take on one newborn vampire, but vampires were fast and if he struck first, it was hard to say if she'd be able to whip up a spell in time to save her life.

Theresa leaned back but the wall was behind her. She had nowhere to go. Cornered. "The betrayer will try to hurt you. And you should know that in previous dealings, I gave him a potion that will protect him from death."

Shane stopped walking. "A potion?"

"Until the potion wears off in a month, you can't kill him." Theresa judged the moment and decided it was time to go before she lost control of the situation. "Believe it or not, I am on your side. I don't want the betrayer to be the victor. When you need me, call on me."

Shane carefully weighed her words. "How?"

Theresa reached deep into the pocket of her black robe and pulled out a small hex bag. "Burn this. I won't be able to resist the pull." She began to put her hood up to leave when Shane thought of another question.

"What does he look like?"

Theresa knew that expression Shane wore. She'd had it a time or two herself. He knew deep in his soul who the betrayer was and just wanted confirmation. "Tall. Skinny. Long, white-blonde hair. Smells like death himself." She put her hood up as she watched realization dawn on Shane's face. At least she accomplished that much. Shane could confront the betrayer now and get him out of her hair. "And he craves power. It's clear that he's jealous of you."

"Jealous?"

"He wants to rule all the vampires. Foolish monster. He wanted to be the one from the Prophecy." And Theresa vanished as quickly as she had the morning at the Bellinz compound.

Shane stood staring at the small hex bag in his hands, allowing his fangs to retract now that the threat was gone.

He'd never seen a hex bag before. It was made of something like burlap and tied with a small string at the top. The whole thing was no bigger than a large grape and he cupped it in his palm. Would he ever find a need to side with witches? And what was he judging anyway? Were they really so much worse than many of the vampires he'd met?

Julianna opened the door and stuck her head inside. She was wearing a robe and her hair was still wet from the shower. "I thought I heard a woman's voice."

Shane stared at his sister, still annoyed with her from earlier and now annoyed at the intrusion. "And so you came barging in?"

She gave him the big sister look. "It didn't sound...amorous."

Shane sat on the bed. "The witch was here."

Julianna came all the way inside his room, horror plastered across her face. "Here? How'd she know where to find you?"

"I suspect it's time we stop underestimating the witches." He squeezed the bag in his hand, sensing its magic.

Luke appeared in the doorway, leaning against the frame, his arms folded across his broad chest. "Witches? Now we have to deal with them too?"

"The betrayer brought them into this, so now they're a player in the game." Shane looked up at his friend. If he was still mad at Luke, he wasn't showing it right now.

"So let me get this straight, we somehow have to stop the Shadow Wars, unite all the vampires *and* placate the witches?" Julianna was still aghast at the news a witch had invaded their compound. She'd seen it at the Bellinz home, but somehow this was more...personal.

"So what do we do?" Luke asked, his eyes hard when he looked at Shane and then soft as he turned his gaze to Julianna. Shane had to acknowledge that he did look at her like she was the rarest of gems. Perhaps he had overreacted earlier.

Shane stood up and crossed to his dresser, the same spot Theresa had been standing in moments before. "We? There's no we. I have to handle this."

Julianna exchanged a look with Luke, and then he stepped into the room. "Oh no. We're in this together. Julianna was the one who resurrected you and I was there when you first used your powers. Like it or not, we're like a weird family. I haven't had anyone to care about in hundreds of years. I'm not leaving either of your sides."

Julianna stood up and grabbed Luke's hand, her eyes on her brother. "Me neither. I've believed in you since before you were reborn. I'll follow you and serve you and protect you until the end of my days. Just tell me what you want me to do."

Shane looked at his sister, then at his best friend. At least there were two people in this crazy world he could trust. "All right, then." He slipped the hex bag in his pocket and grabbed Julianna's shoulders. They looked straight into each other's eyes.

The next step would be a big test for the both of them. "We have to confront the betrayer."

16

Lord Dimas sat in his basement, drinking a glass of O positive splashed with bourbon—his drink of choice. He was happy, and maybe even a little bit proud, that Shane had been able to stop the battle at the Fortis compound. Shane had even managed to convert the little firecracker, Isabelle. Dimas had hoped Shane would have been marked with the Strashni symbol by now, but he knew perfectly well some things couldn't be rushed.

And now he had the disturbing news about the Prudens tribe sneaking away. And going where exactly? And why? It really made no sense.

He swirled his cup, watching the thick red liquid move slowly in his glass. Maybe he should stop worrying. He could take the Strashni and find a new territory too. Hadn't he come from Europe originally anyway? What did California mean to him? Nothing. This was a place he'd ended up in, not his true home. And it was unnatural, all this heat and infernal sunshine.

And what was he going to do about Luke? Clearly Shane liked him. Loved him, even, as a brother. Dimas thought back to a skinny kid with big ears and wished he'd just killed him back then. Why hadn't he? Luke was just an extra complication that Dimas knew he didn't need.

He tossed his head back as he took a deep drink. He swallowed, letting the thick warm liquid slide slowly down his throat, staining his teeth and fangs red. He closed his eyes to feel the blood nourish him just as someone barged in the door to his sanctuary. He stood in anger, ready to reprimand, but it was Julianna. Shane and Luke were right behind her, so Dimas held his tongue.

But they were all starting to get a little too big for their britches. He was still in charge of the Strashni.

"Lord Dimas," Julianna said, bowing her head,

"we need a word with you. It's urgent." She hovered in the doorway, and it was clear she wanted to enter his room. He didn't want her to get too comfortable with barging in, and so he let her stew in the doorway a bit longer.

"With regards to what?" Dimas leaned his head to one side, neither inviting them in nor sending them away. He was relaxed though, seemingly unconcerned with their urgent matter.

"Shane knows who the betrayer is," Julianna blurted out.

Still nonchalant, Dimas held a hand out to punctuate his question. "And why is that urgent? That vampire will meet his own end."

"Oh, cut the shit, Dimas." Luke barged into the room, pushing past Julianna. "A witch was here, in your compound."

This garnered Dimas's attention. He brushed his long hair away from his face as he raised an eyebrow questioningly.

"Yeah. I thought you might be interested in that.

You may be happy to let the betrayer naturally meet his doom, but you can't have witches coming and going as they wish." Luke's nostrils flared as he stared Dimas down. The tension between them was making the room thick and weighted. They were several feet apart, and yet it felt like barely a spark could set them off.

Annoyingly, Dimas said nothing. He looked to the floor so as to avoid Luke's pointed stare. Julianna rushed in and knelt before her Lord. Gently she took the glass from his hand and laid it on the end table nearest to them. She then took both his hands in hers.

"My Lord, we can stop this. Just say the word and Shane will end the betrayer. The witches will stop when they aren't being given our every movement by him." She squeezed his hands in emphasis, and Dimas looked down at her beautiful face. She was so loyal.

Dimas looked up to Shane still standing in the doorway, completely ignoring Luke. "And tomorrow? What happens next? There might always be another betrayer. A good leader must look two or three steps ahead."

Shane didn't answer right away. He folded his arms across his chest and stood tall. After a strategic pause, he said, "What's your plan, Dimas? If you don't care about the betrayer, what do you want the next move to be? I'm not the leader here. You are."

Dimas smiled at that, pulling Julianna up so she stood next to him. He was starting to like Shane. Too bad he had to be friends with Luke. "I just got word that a tribe of vampires was sneaking out of the California territory. I was hoping you might take a team and go after them."

"To what end?" Shane asked.

Dimas's eyes narrowed slightly, but he showed no other emotion. "Find out why. Convince them to stay."

"We'll do it. We'd be happy to." Julianna practically bounced next to Dimas, squeezing his hand again. She was so eager to please Lord Dimas.

Shane was less bullish. "How can we be sure it's not an ambush?"

Luke watched Shane carefully.   His body

language was of someone on guard.

"Why would I send you into an ambush?" Dimas asked casually.

Shane stepped forward. "Why would you care more about a migrating tribe than the vampire among us who is selling our secrets to witches?"

Luke turned straight to Dimas. "You bastard!"

Julianna looked to Dimas and then to Luke and Shane, her eyes wide. "Shane? Why don't you trust in Lord Dimas?"

"Because he's the betrayer." Shane said it so calmly, Julianna almost thought she'd misheard it. But Luke's fangs and claws extended, and she knew something was going down.

Stepping in front of her master, her idol, Julianna said, "No. You are mistaken. You can't trust a witch. She's turning us all against each other. It's not Lord Dimas. He would never betray us."

"Julianna, step aside so I can finally kill this monster," Luke growled. He was seething. Never a born fighter, yet he crouched to rip Dimas's heart right out of his chest.

Shane walked over calmly and gently rested a hand on Luke's arm. "He can't be harmed. The witches gave him a potion to protect him." Shane's eyes stayed glued to Dimas, who said nothing through the whole accusation. He allowed Julianna to vouch for him. "Isn't that right, betrayer?"

Dimas didn't flinch at the words. He just smiled, still standing behind Julianna. "Listen to your sister. You'll get nowhere if you trust witches."

"Something you probably found out the hard way. Never thought she'd come here to warn me, did you?" Shane smiled back. "The thing is, I already knew." Shane walked a couple steps forward, still across the room from Dimas but letting him know he wasn't afraid. Shane's only concern was Julianna, who still stood dangerously close to the betrayer. She still blindly trusted this false idol. "Did you know I can control water now? I imagine earth and wind will come soon, if I practice."

The look of worry creasing Dimas's brow told

Shane that he hadn't heard that piece of information yet. Perhaps Shane and Luke weren't the only vampires who didn't trust the Strashni leader.

"And somehow I've gained the ability of sight. Like, knowing things before they happen or sensing a truth in all the lies. It's not intuition. It's clarity." Shane took another cautious step forward.

Dimas grabbed both Julianna's shoulders, shielding himself behind her. He squeezed her hard. "Don't come any closer."

Julianna was still confused, her heart not allowing her brain to see the truth right before her. "Lord Dimas? Why are you hurting me? Let me go. Shane's just confused. Hexed by witches."

Dimas squeezed tighter and Luke growled next to Shane, still crouched and ready for a fight. He wanted to rip Dimas's hands off Julianna. Shane extended his arm, stopping Luke and trying to keep the situation calm. He needed to get Julianna away. Would fire work on Dimas despite the potion?

The contortion of Dimas's face told Shane

everything he already knew. An internal battle was waging and his usual calm demeanor was beginning to unravel. Fighting to swallow his rage, Dimas spat out, "You think you're special! You're nobody."

Julianna twisted, still held tight in Dimas's grip, trying to understand his words, trying to make sense of something that simply didn't add up to her. "I've seen what he can do, Dimas! He's the one. The boy from the Prophecy!"

"There. Is. No. Prophecy." And the battle was lost. Dimas had lost his cool. His face was no longer a mask of nonchalance. He was full bore mad. Julianna stilled as the words penetrated her mind, realization dawning on her. Luke stared. Only Shane remained stoic. Dimas continued, his words spewing from his mouth like vomit. "I made it all up! You think you're some special chosen one. You're NOTHING!" He laughed, hysterical laughter. His face continuing to morph into chaos and rage.

Julianna's voice was barely a whisper. "What? Why?"

"I set all the game pieces up for me. *I* was supposed to be the chosen one, the one to unite the vampires. The one to rule them all. I set this in motion centuries ago, biding my time. And then you two *children* come along and ruin everything." Dimas was literally spitting now, the anger oozing from every pore.

Shane stepped forward. "You still can. I want none of this. Just give me Julianna. We're the only ones who know anything."

"Come any closer and she dies." Dimas's voice was calm again, his claws extended and his right hand now at Julianna's throat. She looked at her brother, Dimas's betrayal reflected in her eyes. She wasn't afraid. She was hurt and her heart was broken. She had pledged her life to her Lord, doing everything he'd asked. She'd trusted him blindly, and now that trust was crashing down all around her. Nothing hurt worse than the betrayal of someone you'd placed on a pedestal.

"You know I can burn you from here," Shane said simply, stating facts.

"We also both know you can't hurt me," Dimas spewed in response.

"Then let her go and we'll all go our separate ways." Shane spoke softly, like you would to calm a wild animal. Luke was frozen behind him, afraid to make a move that might get Julianna hurt, despite his urge to kill Dimas.

"Sorry." Dimas's eyes went glossy and in an instant Shane knew the decision had been made. "This is all her fault."

With superhuman speed and strength, Dimas ripped Julianna's head from her body and fled out the side door with her head in one hand and her body in the other. In an effort to stop Dimas, Shane shot a fireball in his path, burning the door he left through. A second fireball burned the grass and even singed Dimas's skinny legs as he ran.

"Noooooooooooooooo!" Luke screamed, falling to his knees. "Shane, stop. You'll hurt Julianna!"

"She's already dead, Luke." And when Shane said the words, it all became real. Shane stopped trying to burn Dimas and fell on his knees next to Luke. He stared at the wall, everything feeling surreal. "He killed her."

Luke sobbed loudly and then ran for the burnt-down door. "I'll kill him."

Shane ran to his friend and grabbed his arm. "You can't. You'll only get yourself killed and I can't…" He swallowed the lump that was forming in his throat. "I can't lose you too."

Shane breathed air he didn't need in an effort to overcome his emotions. He had to remain clearheaded, but the pain of witnessing Dimas's murder of his beautiful sister was there all around him, threatening to suffocate him. Shane had very little to lose—barely anything he cared about in this undead life. But Julianna had been one of them. He hated Dimas, but the pain of losing Julianna was overwhelming everything else.

Tears were streaming from Luke's eyes as he tightened his jaw. "When the potion wears off, he's mine."

Shane nodded. Something had happened

between those two years ago, and Shane figured Luke deserved the honor. As long as Dimas was dead, who cared what the means were to that end? "In a few weeks."

"What do we do until then?" Luke asked honestly. His voice was small, hollow. So lost. His pain was emptiness. Shane was forcing him to regroup. Julianna's death wouldn't be in vain. This had to end.

"We plan our revenge, we wait. Just as he did for centuries." Shane saw Dimas's half-finished drink of blood and bourbon. He picked it up, swirled it, and then threw it at the wall. The shattering glass and blood running down in streams did very little to ease the knot of anger and hurt forming from Julianna's murder.

Luke watched Shane. And then he walked over and picked up the lamp that had been next to the glass on the end table. He picked it up and threw it against the wall, letting it shatter next to the blood. They stood there in silence for a moment.

"So what do we do about the Prophecy?" Luke finally asked, breaking the silence.

"We fulfill it," Shane said matter-of-factly.

"Shane, you are powerful, but there IS no chosen one. There isn't even a real prophecy. You heard Dimas. That hunk of shit made the whole thing up, just as I'd always suspected."

Shane turned to his friend. "I know that and you know that, but no one else besides Dimas does. We want to get back at Dimas? This is the best way. I fulfill his dreams and he watches it happen." Shane's eyes darkened, a flash of Julianna's head severed from her body entering his mind and stirring his emotions. "Then we kill him."

Luke looked back at the bloodstained wall. His face was a tangle of emotions and memories. "He slaughtered my whole tribe. That bastard," Luke finally said, the truth of the past finally ready to be told. "Dimas. This is centuries ago. Long before the Strashni although I've always suspected he did the same to come into power here." Shane watched Luke head to the small couch and flop down in sheer emotional exhaustion. "I had barely been a vampire maybe as long as you. I was still thinking this life was a gift. Women couldn't resist me. I was immortal, strong, could see in the dark." Luke shook his head at the stolen version of himself as a young vampire. "And trusting. Stupidly trusting. Dimas told me he had a proposal for us. I believed him and welcomed him in. He slaughtered them in front of me, drinking the blood of Simone, the woman who had turned and resurrected me. She was like a mother to me."

Shane felt his eyes well up with emotion, not only for the loss of his own dear sister but also the loss he felt for his best friend. Dimas had murdered many things in his time. "He drank my maker's blood right in front of me just to torture me. As if the betrayal wasn't enough. As if their slaughter wasn't enough. He had to crush my spirit too." Luke stared at the floor where the memories had been dancing before his eyes. His pained expression stabbed Shane's heart. "We are all vampires living among vampires. Hell, I've even encountered witches. But Dimas is the first true monster I've ever met."

Luke looked up at Shane, his eyes dry but the pain still clearly bubbling just beneath the surface, wounds both old and new. "It's my fault, Shane. Everything. This is all my fault."

Shane shook his head. "It's not."

"He stood before me that day. I had a wooden stake in my hand. But I couldn't do it. I had the chance to kill that murdering bastard, and I didn't. I couldn't."

"Dimas is responsible for his own actions."

"He laughed at me. When I couldn't do it. He laughed at me and left."

A noise at the basement door put Shane's senses back on high alert. Luke still just stared at the floor. Shane watched as Elias flew in, worry on his face.

"I thought I heard a crash. Everything okay?" Elias looked at Shane and Luke and then saw the burnt-up side door that Dimas had fled through. "What happened?"

Elias was a good soldier and Shane needed those, so he decided to be honest. "Dimas was the betrayer. When we confronted him, he murdered my sister and fled with her body."

The shock was etched across Elias' face. "What?"

Luke stood somberly. His heart was broken, but he knew there was work to be done. And he would fight until the death for Shane. "So what's the plan, Shane? I know you've got one. How do we fulfill the Dark Prophecy and unite the vampires?"

Shane looked at Luke and then at Elias. He would need them both. "I'm going to unite them against a common enemy. The one parting gift Dimas gave us. I'm going to unite all the vampires against the witches."

17

Under the cover of a dark night, the tribe of Prudens vampires moved quickly through a forest of trees. With a bird's eye view, it would look like a line of ants working toward a summer picnic. Some were hunched over and sneaking. Others felt no need to hide, holding their head high. All had chosen to leave the territory of the Shadow Wars behind.

"I'm hungry," a long dark-haired vampire named Bronwyn grumbled.

"Find an animal to feed on," Johann, the Prudens leader, instructed. He was exhausted, the decision to leave weighing heavily on his mind. For centuries he'd fought with other tribes for a tiny piece of a big state. Protecting hunting grounds was thankless work. He decided it wasn't worth the fight anymore. Especially now that the Dark Prophecy was coming true. And he hadn't forced anyone to come with him, although he knew the loyalty to one's tribe was powerful. He looked down at the Prudens mark forever decorating his forearm. A simple upside-down triangle. Simple and powerful.

"I need human flesh," Bronwyn moaned. She was an old vampire, with paper-thin skin. She still found it hard to wear clothes that didn't button up to her throat. And showing ankles? Forget it. She might be in a blouse and jeans, but a lady never reveals her goods to just anyone.

"And why are we sneaking away like common criminals?" Carmine yelled from the center of the pack. He was one of the tribe's most esteemed warriors. Tall, strong, built like a football player. Prudens members trusted him and looked up to him in every way.

"No one has to come who doesn't want to," Johann repeated, completely misunderstanding the complaining.

"We just want to find a village of humans we can

feed on," Bronwyn whined.

"We'll make it to a small town before morning." Johann stopped walking and turned back to his tribe. They all stopped to listen to him. He didn't need to yell—with their superhuman hearing his whispers would carry on the breeze. "If we like it there, we can stay. There are very few vampire tribes in this region. Most are up near Seattle."

The Prudens tribe murmured amongst themselves. Johann smiled, yellow teeth glowing in the moonlight. His hair was long, but in a way that suited him. He was tall and well-built though not as good a fighter as some. His tribe trusted him for his wisdom. He was one of the oldest vampires in the tribe and had seen his share of battle and survival.

"But is the human population enough around here to keep us fed?" Carmine again.

"We may have to take out a tribe or two, but yes, I believe we can live here comfortably for centuries." Johann nodded to Carmine. If he could convince Carmine, that would settle much of the unrest. Carmine seemed to soften and didn't argue further. Johann would take that as a good sign. "But we must keep going. We don't want to be trapped here come sunlight."

He turned again to the path they were following, beginning to lead his tribe to their new promised land. They wove between trees, flora and fauna, occasionally hearing the rustle of a woodland creature. They climbed a small hill, and Johann paused at the sight before him.

Twenty women in dark robes with the hoods pulled up stood blocking the path they followed. Johann knew who they were but hadn't predicted this unforeseen event. *Witches.* How on earth could they have possibly known the tribe was here?

One witch stepped forward onto the path, lowering her hood. She stood a few feet from Johann, and all the Prudens vampires began gathering up around him to see what was blocking the path. Bronwyn hissed in Johann's ear when she realized what stood before them.

Elyse stood in the moonlight, her ash-blonde hair pulled back tight. She seemed confident, but Johann couldn't figure out why. He could rip her throat out in ten seconds. And they were hungry.

Elyse smiled, but it wasn't warm, it was predatory. "And where could you be slithering off to like varmints?"

This struck a nerve with Carmine and he growled from somewhere behind Johann.

"Let me eat her," Bronwyn hissed, her body pushing up to Johann as she fought the urge to feast on the witches before her.

Elyse lifted her chin as if inviting Bronwyn to try, but she said nothing. Johann was completely confused. These witches stood before a tribe of hungry vampires and acted as if the *vampires* should be afraid.

"What is it you want? Why have you followed us? We have no quarrel with your kind," Johann shouted into the night. He splayed his arms in an attempt to keep the vampires in his tribe calm. But they were anything but, restlessly pacing and growling behind him as they imagined the taste of witches across their lips and pouring down into their empty bellies.

"We're here to kill you," Elyse answered honestly.

A few vampires growled the more. A few others licked their lips in a dramatic display. Johann had to laugh. "Twenty witches? Against a tribe of starving vampires?" He shook his head at their audacity. "I'll give you one chance to get out of our way."

Elyse looked back at the witches behind her. They still stood in a line, black robes on, hoods up. When Elyse turned back, she stepped forward, closing the space between herself and Johann. The other witches stepped forward, following suit.

Johann sighed, blowing his long bangs out of his face with the gust of his heavy breath. "Very well, then."

He had barely lowered his arms with the symbol that said they could have their way when Bronwyn had roared past him, fangs bared and glistening in the moonlight. Other vampires began their attack, as well, but watched as Elyse lifted an arm and pushed at the air.

Without even touching her, she lifted Bronwyn and threw her to the edge of the path, only a few feet from the trees. Casually, Elyse strolled over to where Bronwyn had landed, stunned but not really hurt. Elyse pulled a wooden stake from her robe, polished at one end and then sharpened like a pencil at the other. She'd barely exerted any energy before she'd plunged the stake into Bronwyn's heart, surprise utterly pasted across Bronwyn's face, and the old vampire shriveled up even further, a dusty bag of bones at Elyse's feet.

Turning to the other Prudens vampires, many of whom had halted when they saw Bronwyn destroyed with barely a finger lifted, Elyse asked, "Who's next?"

Her brazen attitude and her general witchy ways were already enough to incite the Prudens, but Johann's battle cry of "Avenge Bronwyn!" stirred them all from their stupefied state. Most of the vampires had never encountered witches and the ones who had thought of them as nuisances and nothing more. Watching them murder one of their own kind? They'd never thought it possible.

The Prudens vampires ran at the witches with full force. Most of the front line never made it there. They were tossed like rag dolls by witchcraft alone—no witch had laid a finger on them. A few made it past the ones being tossed, and some even got a bite or two in, but soon met the same fate and were tossed into the woods.

"They're here," Elyse announced and Johann followed her line of sight to a spot down the trail behind him. Many more witches in black robes closed in behind the Prudens tribe. They were surrounded. "The Portland Coven."

Johann turned back to see one of his own, a vampire who had been tearing the flesh off one of the witches, get a stake right through the heart. "Rip their arms off! So they can't stake you!" Johann shouted his instructions. But vampires weren't always calculating killers. So used to dominating their prey, they hadn't really honed in skills of cunning if they weren't compelling their victims.

Carmine saw Elyse in his sights and he wanted

her blood. His own boiled with rage when he thought about her daring to attack his tribe. He would relish every bite of flesh torn from bone, licking the blood until only a pile of shiny white bones remained. He snarled as he approached. He'd watched her toss his other tribe members, so he ducked when she waved in his direction. It worked! He remained planted on the ground. He weaved and moved his head as he approached and was able to get close enough to tackle her.

On all fours above her, pinning down her shoulders, his fangs were inches from her pretty face. But he was a good soldier and so he followed Johann's instructions, biting a huge chunk of her left arm off and swallowing it in one lump. He licked the blood off his lips as she screamed in agony. Carmine went in for another bite—this time planning to remove what was left—and he froze in shock. He watched the flesh he'd torn off grow back and become whole again.

Elyse began laughing beneath him.

Carmine became blind with rage. Now she

mocked him? He could think of nothing else besides ripping her heart from her chest. As if in slow motion, he watched Elyse pull another stake from her robe, and he easily flung it away and then bit her hand off. She swiped her other arm at him and he flew back, hitting a tree near the path and causing it to shake violently, leaves falling all around him. He gathered his bearings and ran back toward her, noticing as he ran how her hand was growing back again.

Johann watched it all with growing concern. Even when witches were attacked, they healed immediately. Not one witch had fallen, but vampires were getting thrown and staked all around him. The rear flanks were faring no better. The Portland witches must have taken the same potion. Only members of his tribe were suffering casualties. He had to think of a way to defeat them—and quickly—or they wouldn't survive the night.

18

"Isabelle, will you talk to Damian?" Shane asked as he pulled on a long black leather coat, preparing for the confrontation ahead. "I'll get Regina and the Bellinz."

"And tell them what, exactly? The Fortis are many things, but compassionate isn't one of them." Isabelle swooped her long black hair up into a tight ponytail. "They couldn't care less about another tribe of vampires being slaughtered."

"I'm not asking anyone for compassion. It's just survival." Shane stood up straight, looking into Isabelle's eyes. Damn, she was like an exotic flower that was beautiful to see but deadly if you got too close.

Isabelle raised an eyebrow at Shane, not completely buying his reasoning.

"And good old-fashioned revenge," Shane smiled. Isabelle smiled back. Now he was speaking her language. "The witches have used everything they can against us, completely unprovoked. If we don't stop them, they'll keep coming after us. They know where all our compounds are now. This is our one chance because we actually know where they'll be."

"All right, all right." Isabelle swiped the air to stop him from chattering on and on. "I never said I wouldn't do it."

He pulled her close and kissed her forehead. She took the opportunity to sucker punch him in the ribs. Smiling up at him she said, "I told you not to leave your mid-section too exposed."

Shane smiled back. "What I lack in basic fighting skills I make up for by throwing fireballs."

"There is that," Isabelle responded. Shane started to go around her, heading for the front door of the Strashni compound. "And Luke and Elias will meet us there?"

He opened the door and stood there, the cool

night air behind him and the sound of crickets somewhere on the porch. "They have their own mission. But they'll be there." He pulled up his collar and stepped out onto the porch. He gently patted his pocket to make sure the hex bag from Theresa was still there.

"Shane." Isabelle's tone was uncharacteristically soft. He turned to look over his shoulder. "I'm sorry about your sister."

Shane nodded and then burst off the porch in a surge of vampire speed.

Isabelle grabbed the keys from the key ring near the front door and waltzed into the garage. There, in the spotlight of the overhead light, sat a shiny red Ducati. She might be willing to do anything for Shane, but she'd be damned before she'd do it on foot. Not with this beauty calling to her.

Roaring the engine to life, Isabelle rode the motorcycle out of the garage and headed for the hills where her old tribe still partied. She burst forth with speed of her own, but she was doing it in style. The wind all around her invigorated her and she knew she wouldn't let her new Lord, soon to be the leader of all vampires, down. She was on a mission to get Damian and the Fortis tribe to join Shane and all the other tribes in the Cascade Mountains to defeat witches.

And she wasn't about to fail.

†††

Kara knocked on the bathroom door where her sister was holed up doing her hair and make-up or something. "Seriously, Emily? You've been in there for an hour."

"I'm almost done, Kara. You'll understand when you're older. Then you won't always want to look like a tomboy," Emily shouted back through the closed door.

Kara let her shoulders fall in defeat. Older sisters were complete pains in the ass. She stood there for a moment imagining all the ways she would get back at her sister when suddenly there was a gust of wind behind her.

She turned around in the hallway to see a tall,

extremely handsome man. A strange man. Kara stared, confused but not scared.

"Come quick. It's your mother," the handsome man said.

Kara rolled her eyes at the stranger. "My mother's dead."

"Stepmother then. She needs you. Come with me." The handsome man extended a hand and Kara looked at it, then folded her arms across her chest.

"Do you think I'm stupid enough to just go with you?" Kara leaned on one hip defiantly.

A second man with long black hair emerged from Theresa and Richard's bedroom. "Just compel her already. Two teenagers shouldn't be this hard to kidnap."

She wasn't sure what was going on, but suddenly Kara wasn't so cocky. "Compel her" didn't sound natural in any way. She turned and started to run, but the handsome man grabbed her arm and looked deep into her eyes. She tried to pull away but then found that she didn't want to. Her muscles melted into his arms and her knees gave out beneath her. The handsome man lifted her and cradled her in his arms. She rested her head on his shoulder. He was so handsome and warm. Did she ever want him to put her down again?

"Where's your sister?" the dark-haired man asked.

Kara continued to gaze at the handsome man holding her but found herself unable to resist answering his question. "In the bathroom there." She gestured to the closed door.

With one pound of a fist, the door caved in and Emily screamed. Kara giggled. She found it funny that she'd wanted her sister out of there, wanted revenge even, and here it was in the form of two strange men. Had she conjured them? Was this all her doing in an attempt to punish her sister? She giggled all the more as the long-haired man picked Emily up and tossed her over his shoulder. She kept screaming, so Kara watched as the man touched her temple and Emily fell silent as if she were in a deep sleep.

This made Kara giggle again.

With the two girls in tow, Luke and Elias bolted from Theresa's bedroom, jumping from the balcony that overlooked the ocean and landing in the soft sand of the Ventura beach. It was a long way to go to the Oregon border, so they kicked into vampire speed and left Ventura behind.

Emily slept the whole way, bouncing on Elias's shoulder. Kara watched carefully. She felt heavy and drugged, but she also felt intrigued. Maybe the boring life she'd been tired of living wasn't so boring after all. The night had just become very intriguing. She rested her head on her handsome captor's shoulder and watched the world whiz by at unnatural speeds for someone on foot.

Very intriguing indeed.

†††

Up in the Cascades, vampires were still getting thrown and staked, while witches remained unharmed. Or if they happened to be harmed, they quickly recovered and resumed their offensive. It wasn't the bloodiest battlefield Johann had ever been on, but it was still an annihilation. Bodies of vampires littered the hiking trail, shriveled up like decayed mummies. He could practically see the dust emanating from their bodies every time they were staked.

He'd tried to attack their leader at one point, and it proved fruitless and served to remind him how powerless he was. It wasn't a position he was used to being in. He wasn't even convinced retreat was an option. If the witches found them here, they could find them anywhere they went.

Johann grabbed the dozen vampires closest to him and drew them near. They were surrounded on all sides by witches fighting other Prudens vampires and he didn't see an easy route to escape, but he somehow envisioned safety in numbers. They couldn't possibly throw all twelve of us, could they?

And then a strange sound echoed in the distance.

Johann heard it first and he stood up straight,

trying to hear over the sounds of battle. Slowly, the Portland witches in the rear stopped fighting. The vampires stopped being thrown. They heard it too.

Someone was coming. Multiple someones were running up the trail.

Johann couldn't imagine this night getting any worse, but so far nothing had gone as planned. Could all of this have been orchestrated by vampires conspiring with witches? He'd heard rumors about a betrayer among vampires—they all had. Had some tribe had a personal vendetta?

The one thing that gave him some degree of confidence was that at least they knew how to fight vampires. He crouched low, fangs and claws extended, preparing for a new foe. The dozen vampires huddled near him took his lead and emulated him.

A blonde vampire in a long black trench coat marched up the hill, hundreds of vampires behind him. Johann immediately recognized Regina, the Bellinz Queen, right at his shoulder. One of the Portland witches sensed the blonde as a threat and lifted her arms as if to throw him as she'd done so many others. Without even a glance in her direction, he held his hand palm out toward her. And nothing happened. Had his hand blocked her spell? With his other arm he waved wildly at the air and a large bubble of water came flying toward them. As if it were tethered to the blonde vampire by some unseen string, it flew over all their heads and went straight like a missile to the witch who had tried to toss him. The bubble of water engulfed her and then shot straight back up into the air, the witch inside it, struggling for air, drowning in the floating water.

"Stand down, witches. I'm only here to talk," Shane announced, his voice booming in the calm night.

"Let our sister go," an evil voice shouted from somewhere amongst the Portland witches.

With the hand that wasn't controlling the water in the air with the witch inside, Shane summoned a fireball. "I know you've all taken a potion that prevents us from killing you, but I assure you it will hurt like hell to burn from head to toe like your ancestors did."

"Let her go or I stake this monster," another

witch from the gathering said, holding a stake to a downed vampire's heart.

Shane cocked his head to the side and then tossed a flame at the wooden stake. It turned to ash in a matter of seconds. There was a hushed murmur throughout the ranks of both witches and vampires. Knowing he'd displayed his power, he let the water bubble drop to the ground, none too gently. A soaking witch coughed and sputtered on the ground as a couple of her witchy "sisters" came to her aid.

"Aw, man, you didn't wait for me!" Isabelle came bounding up the hill with another hundred vampires behind her, Damian at her side. Shane went to her and hugged her.

He then turned back to the battlefield. "I know you were sent here by Theresa," Shane announced. "Leave now and this goes no further."

Elyse knew she couldn't let it end like this. She stormed past Johann toward Shane. "We don't answer to you and we're still more powerful than the rest of the vampires here."

"Let's see what Theresa would say about how you've done tonight, shall we?" Shane pulled the hex bag from his pocket and held it out in the middle of the palm of his hand. Elyse, recognizing what it was, recoiled at the thought. There was fear in her eyes, but she tried to hide it.

Johann watched all of this with fascination and confusion. "Are you the one from the Dark Prophecy?" he stammered toward Shane.

"I am," Shane nodded, his voice solid with confidence. "And any vampire who follows me is under my protection."

"Summon her. Go ahead. She'll see how naïve she was to think she could ever partner with you." Elyse spit the words, anger clearly lining her forehead.

"Can I kill her, my Lord?" Isabelle asked.

"Unfortunately, no," Shane responded to Isabelle. To Elyse he repeated, "This is your last warning. Leave now or I summon Theresa."

"Do it," Elyse spit again. A few other witches echoed her sentiment.

His eyes locked on Elyse's as he summoned a flame to the palm of his hand and lit the hex bag. They all watched as it turned to ash before their eyes in the palm of Shane's hand.

When the hex bag was nothing but ash in Shane's palm, a burst of smoke appeared right before Shane. When it cleared, Theresa stood in the clearing. She wasn't wearing her black robe like the other witches. She was dressed professionally, her hair pulled high on her head, as if she'd been summoned from the boardroom in the middle of the night.

"Therese St. Claire?" Johann couldn't hide his shock.

Theresa took in the situation all around her. She'd expected Elyse to quickly and quietly take care of the Prudens. A battle with the Chosen One wasn't exactly her short-term game plan. Clearly things had gone awry.

Calmly she walked over to Johann and patted his cheek. He pulled back from her touch as if it disgusted him. "My dear friend, Johann. It has been a while, hasn't it? Remember when we were both on trial together? Imagine." Theresa turned back to the larger group as if telling a fun folktale. "We were both on trial for witchcraft." Theresa giggled. "Of course, in my case they were right. Although they would never have the chance to punish me for it. But Johann? They mistook his nightly feedings for witchcraft." She shook her head. "He could only wish to be so lucky. I wonder what they would have done had they known the truth?" She giggled, as though human fear of monsters were some hilarious joke.

"Therese. Why would you order your witches to murder my tribe?" Johann asked. He truly looked shocked and hurt, which surprised Shane, who watched their interaction closely.

"I go by Theresa now. It's so California, don't you think? And don't take it personally. Do I get offended every time you drink the blood of a fellow human? But it is good to see someone from the old world."

"Theresa," Elyse pleaded with her leader. "We

were winning. Look how many vampires we killed tonight. But Shane showed up and summoned you. He's our enemy after all."

Theresa smiled at Elyse. If she was angry, she didn't show it. She walked past Elyse and straight up to Shane. "Is this true, dear Shane? Are we unable to make a truce?"

"It's not true. I believe we can come to an agreement. I've confronted the betrayer and he ran. It's him that I want." Shane gestured to the vampires all around him. "And protection for any vampire who follows me. That's it."

Theresa smirked at Shane. It was predatory, malicious. She didn't look warm and friendly; she looked ready to squash a bug under her shoe. "Then let's talk terms, sweet Shane."

19

"You leave us tonight. Now. And if the betrayer comes to you again, you hand him over to me," Shane stipulated.

"And in return?" Theresa asked calmly, her well-manicured hands on her well-dressed hips.

Shane shrugged. "Name your price."

"Your power." Theresa said plainly. Vampires and witches alike gasped in surprise. "You let me strip you of your abilities, and I'll leave every one of you alone and even help you find the betrayer."

Shane watched Theresa closely. He understood her perspective. Vampires were her enemy, and he was the most powerful adversary. But then she would tip the scales in her favor. And he couldn't trust her anyway. And he might barely be able to admit it to himself, but he was growing fond of his newfound skills. They were part of him. He really didn't know how to be anything other than what he was in this new life. He couldn't let her take that away.

The crystal-clear night sky had suddenly become thick with anticipation. Up here in these mountains, there was very little pollution. The trees were abundant, providing shelter and food to nature's gifts. It was so pure in its landscape that the dubious deals being discussed in her foreground were causing a tainting of sorts. A breeze picked up and tossed Shane's sandy blonde hair. He felt as if it were trying to tell them to be on their way.

Take your business elsewhere. Evil and monsters have no place in this beautiful and natural landscape.

Luke was the only other person here, and he was hiding way in the back, who knew the Prophecy was mere propaganda. All other vampire eyes that landed on him *believed* in him, just as Julianna had. He winced momentarily at the fleeting thought of his sister.

The only person who had ever loved him both as human and vampire, and she'd given her life—and his—for her belief in him.

If Theresa wanted a fight, then so be it.

Shane stepped forward, closing the gap between himself and Theresa. "Your price is too high."

Isabelle sighed loudly, as if she'd been afraid he was going to say yes.

"Then no deal tonight," and Theresa pushed her arms forward and a bolt of electricity flew from her fingertips toward Shane.

"No!" Isabelle shouted and ran in front of Shane pushing him out of the way. She was struck by the bolt intended for Shane, and she convulsed with its energy, her eyes rolling back.

"Isabelle!" Shane got up from the dirt and pushed Theresa back with the force of her own electricity. Theresa flew backward.

And then the whole scene erupted anew.

Witches were tossing vampires and pulling out stakes. Vampires were biting and tearing the flesh of witches and then watching it regenerate. Shane scanned the scene, burning every stake to ash that he saw. Without their primary weapon they could toss vampires, but the vampires would be as unharmed as the witches were.

The likelihood of stalemate ended nothing. Witches and vampires kept battling. Shane helped Isabelle to her feet.

"Let me have the leader," Isabelle huffed out the words. Her face was charred and her hair frayed, but being electrocuted did nothing to stop her. She looked as ferocious as she always did. Shane admired her warrior spirit.

"You'll be more helpful protecting other vampires." Shane nodded toward Damian, who was being tossed around like a ragdoll helplessly.

Isabelle growled. She was exasperated both at the bitchy witch and the perpetual weakness of Damian. Fueled by anger, Isabelle ran at vampire speed toward the witch that was attacking Damian and jumped on her back, gnawing away at her neck, the blood dripping down Isabelle's chin. Its coppery smell and sticky sweetness worked like a battery that reenergized her, and she gnawed, chewed, swallowed, savored. The witch tried to toss Isabelle as she had Damian, but she couldn't send the spell over her shoulder. She tried and kept missing.

And Theresa was dusting herself off and smiling at Shane. They watched each other for a moment. Shane had had a back-up plan prepared in case they couldn't negotiate a truce. He just needed to create a pause in the fighting so he could present Theresa with door number two.

Meanwhile she ran at him, on the offensive again, seemingly no desire to talk. She shot her bolts again in his direction, and he created a wall of fire in return. Their powers collided, a barricade of fire and electricity between them. Frustrated, she lowered her bolt. Shane did the same with his firepower. She tried to toss him with a flail of her arms. He blocked it with his own.

From the corner of his eye, he saw another stake

and burnt it to ash in the witch's hand.

Theresa yelled in frustration and then spun, collecting electricity that rained down on her from the sky, a sky that moments ago had held nothing more than a light breeze. She was gathering lightning, calling on the elements. She was a very powerful witch. No other witch here came close to being able to do what Theresa was doing. Electricity sparked from her face, arms, and hands. She snarled at Shane and then shoved the full brunt of her power at him. This time it pushed through his attempt to block her with fire. He was hit with a bolt and tossed backward. The pain was most intense at his shoulder where it had hit, but it radiated out in waves to every crevice of his body. He fought to stay conscious as the pain wracked his nerve endings.

Without getting up he called to water. Water in the sky, water in a nearby stream, dewdrops beginning to form on tree leaves all around. And he threw it at Theresa. He knew water would amplify the electricity she had coursing through her. And when she screamed, he knew it had had its intended effect. Theresa was shaking from her own electrocution. Thank goodness for high school chemistry where he'd learned what a powerful conductor water was for electricity.

Holding his shoulder, he got up slowly, his legs painful and weak beneath him. Theresa was recovering, as well. She held her arms up to the sky, summoning some other element to inflict pain upon her opponents.

All around him, witches were putting up a good fight against such amazing predators. None were as powerful as Theresa, but many were holding their own or even winning. They all bounced back quickly—no mortal wounds could be made. This would go on forever and no one could be victorious.

"Enough!" Shane shouted with his arms extended, and as he did, a burst of energy flew from him, expanding out in a radius where he was the epicenter. The wave hit everyone in its wake, and they were knocked back. The scene it left behind was one of dominos falling. Vampires on top of witches, witches on top of vampires, all forced to the ground by the shock wave Shane had sent.

Well, this is new.

But the stunned reaction of all those on the ground, Theresa among them, was just the opening Shane needed.

"Elias!" Shane called over his shoulder, his eyes never leaving Theresa's. She watched him warily in return, skeptical of what he would do now. His show of power had surprised her.

From the back of the swarm of vampires, all of which were now beginning to stand again and watch the scene unfold, a tall dark-haired warrior vampire marched to the front. In his clutches was a young, human girl, fighting futilely with her captor and crying incessantly. It was virtually the only sound anyone was making.

Everyone watched, curious what the next move was.

Theresa recognized Emily at once and smiled to herself. He thought to use her as leverage! She admired Shane more than ever now. But his efforts would be useless. Emily was fodder to her. In this real-life game of chess, she was nothing but a pawn.

Elias yanked the girl to the clearing where Shane stood, a few feet from Theresa. Theresa stood, saying nothing.

"We just want you to leave," Shane growled, still reeling from the smoldering pain in his shoulder.

"And we want unnatural creatures to die," Theresa responded. She didn't look at Emily.

"We don't want to hurt your daughter," Shane said, "but we will."

As if to highlight the point, Elias dug his claws into Emily's arms and she shrieked in pain.

"*Step*daughter," Theresa corrected. She waved her hand in front of her face dismissively. "And I couldn't care less what you do with her. She means nothing to me."

Shane nodded to Elias, and he stretched Emily's neck out as straight as it could go, she fighting as hard (and uselessly) as she could. Elias elongated his fangs and lowered them to centimeters from Emily's throat.

Shane looked up at Theresa, who stood with her

hands on her hips. Shane could see an expression that looked like she didn't care about Emily's fate. And, of course, she didn't.

"Do it," Theresa goaded. A wicked smiled crossed her lips.

This wasn't working as planned so he turned to Elias and whispered, "Let her go."

Elias shoved Emily to the ground, and she scrambled on her hands and knees to Theresa. Theresa ignored her as she would the wind. Elyse came over to Theresa and Emily and offered solidarity, although she didn't extend a hand to the teenager shaking in fear at their feet.

"Luke!" Shane called out.

"Are we done with your mind games? Don't get me wrong, no one loves mind games as much as I do, but I came here tonight to slaughter vampires. I'm not leaving until I do."

Shane said nothing, just stared at her sternly as out of the crowds came a tall and handsome Luke, bringing Kara to the front. Unlike her sister, she didn't fight. She even looked curious, as if this were all some movie or video game.

And realization dawned on Theresa. Kara she had cared about. She had had plans to teach her the craft, induct her into the Harbor Coven. Of course he had brought both girls. Why hadn't she expected that? Theresa's lips twitched as she thought about losing her protégé, but she recovered quickly. Only Shane, watching her intensely and sensing her truth with his power, saw her falter for a fraction of a second.

Yes, Theresa had had plans for Kara but she was willing to sacrifice her for the greater good. There'd be other girls. There always were. She wouldn't tip her hand to Shane, let him see her weakness. She admired his feeble attempt to exploit her emotions, it was a game Theresa played exceptionally well. But she'd had centuries to hone her craft. Shane was a novice.

She looked down her nose at him. "Kill her."

"Oh, we don't plan to kill her," Shane said just as he nodded to Luke.

Luke bit Kara in the neck and drained her of her

blood right before Theresa's and Emily's eyes. Emily screamed but did nothing for she was frozen from fear. She prayed that this was all some nightmare she would wake up from, drenched in sweat but relieved to know it wasn't real. Kara, however, didn't fight. Her eyes stayed locked on Theresa, and she never begged for mercy or shed one tear.

Damn, what a waste. She would have been a magnificent witch!

And then Luke bit his own wrist and forced Kara to drink his blood and everything changed. Theresa realized what Shane had meant. They *weren't* planning to kill her. They were planning to *turn* her.

Theresa screamed and a single tear finally fell from her eye. Death she could handle, but her protégé turned into a monster? That was beyond the unthinkable. At Theresa's reaction, Emily became hysterical, screaming, sobbing and hiccupping.

Theresa rarely wore her true emotions anywhere to be seen, so her pain alerted Elyse. She couldn't stand idly by.

"Kill them," she shouted to the witches. "Kill them all."

Shane lifted a hand and sent a fireball at Elyse. She caught fire and burned from head to toe, flailing her arms and screaming from the pain. She looked like a burning bush trying to put itself out.

"Elyse!" Theresa screamed. She fell to her knees, staring at Shane. First Kara and then Elyse? There were only so many people she cared about in this world. Theresa summoned electricity from the sky, but she didn't use it. She felt defeated, even as she crackled and fumed at Shane's feet. "Put her out. And we'll go."

Shane tossed water on Elyse and the flames died out. Her hair was black and matted from the water, her flesh charred beyond recognition. She shook in the clearing, convulsing from pain and humiliation.

"No one could win here tonight anyway," Shane shouted.

Theresa slowly stood, her eyes alight with the fires of rage. She took a deep breath and spoke calmly. "Fuck. You."

Her hair was no longer the pinnacle of perfection, her dress was torn from battle, her face was contorted with the rage she couldn't keep at bay. But she knew this game well. Push it tonight and more would lose.

Regroup, recalculate and live to fight another day.

As she picked Emily up from the ground, she vowed silently that the *Chosen One* would pay. And she would make it long, drawn out and painful. "Witches, disperse."

With Emily tucked into her side, Theresa disappeared. And then, one by one each witch vanished into the thin air, a charred and shaking Elyse among them.

Satisfied that the fighting had ceased for at least one day, Shane turned to Luke. "Take her back near the Strashni compound. Bury her in the backyard so when she resurrects, we can train her."

"You *want* that bitch's offspring?" Luke asked incredulously.

Shane nodded. "This isn't a sprint. It's a marathon. Neither the betrayer nor Theresa is dead. This young vampire may still serve a purpose."

Johann approached Shane, trembling with shock from all he'd witnessed and fear of what was still potentially to come. "Thank you for coming. We'd have been massacred without you."

"We're one now." Shane put a hand on Johann's shoulder. "Anyone who follows me is tribeless. All the vampires united. Someone attacks one of us, they fight all of us. We must remember who the real enemies are and not spend our lives fighting one another."

"So it's true? The Dark Prophecy has been fulfilled." Johann's eyes were filled with wonder.

Shane and Luke exchanged a look. And then Luke stood, cradling Kara's body. "It would appear so," Luke said to Johann. "Shane is the one from the Prophecy and he has united all the vampires. You saw tonight how powerful he is."

"I have," Johann whispered and then knelt before Shane. All the remaining Fortis vampires from

Johann's tribe followed suit and did the same. Soon, the Strashni, Bellinz and Prudens vampires all did the same.

"Tell everyone you know," Luke shouted to all the kneeling vampires. "Shane is your new leader and anyone who follows him is under his protection."

"WITCH!" someone screamed from up the hill. Shane ran toward where the voice was coming from and saw a young girl, early twenties, hiding amongst the trees. She looked frightened, small, her round eyes wide with the fear of being surrounded by her mortal enemy.

Isabelle came jogging up to Shane's side. "Shall I dispatch her for you?" Instinctively she licked her lips and cracked her knuckles.

Without taking his eyes off the pretty young witch with the soft brown hair, Shane answered Isabelle. "No." He stepped forward toward the girl. He was surprised she didn't step back or run or hide. She looked frightened and skittish. She watched him as closely as he watched her.

"I'm not going to hurt you." Shane spoke softly and moved slowly, as if approaching a wild animal.

"What is your name?"

"Camilla," she answered confidently, her voice not giving away any of the fear her eyes had shown. And the sound was like music to Shane's ears. She didn't look like a witch to him. She looked like a beautiful, young woman. Her skin was as smooth as cream, kissed by the sun to a dark tan. She couldn't be more than twenty-five.

"Camilla," he repeated, still approaching slowly. "Did your coven leave you? Do you have a way to get back home?"

She shook her head and then took a bold step toward Shane. "I chose not to go."

Shane stopped, suddenly skeptical.

Isabelle spoke the words Shane had been grappling with internally. "It's a trap, Shane."

Camilla shook her head again. "Theresa kidnapped me when I was sixteen. She made me a witch, but it wasn't anything I chose. I am choosing this. Your power. It's like nothing I've ever seen a witch do."

"You can't trust her," Isabelle said again, but less

confidently as she watched Shane's face. He looked intoxicated and Isabelle wasn't entirely sure he wasn't bewitched.

He closed his eyes for a moment before announcing, "She's telling the truth." He stepped forward one more time and extended his hand. She slipped hers into his. "You can stay with us for now. You can't ever go back to Theresa after this."

Under hooded eyes, Camilla said, "I know." She stood close to him and he could hear her heartbeat. He could smell the sweat upon her skin. He wasn't completely sure he wouldn't try to either kiss her full lips or bite her smooth neck. Hand in hand, he pulled her out of the trees and back to the congregation of vampires awaiting his orders.

"Get to one of the compounds in California. It is nearly daybreak. You'll need shelter. We'll figure out the plans for hunting next nightfall," Shane explained. Vampires started leaving, heading south.

"Meet you at the Strashni compound." Luke indicated the girl in his arms. Shane knew he would do precisely as Shane had asked.

Shane nodded to his loyal friend.

"Are you coming?" Isabelle asked Shane when she saw he wasn't moving as fast as the other vampires.

"I can walk in the sunlight, so I'm in no rush," Shane smiled, looking at Camilla, still holding her hand.

Isabelle snorted and rolled her eyes. "Of course you can." She shook her head and then took off with a burst of vampire speed.

20

"How many days do we wait?" Shane asked Luke, squinting in the morning sun. Luke stood in the doorway, under the awning away from the sun's rays.

"Two or three. The transformation doesn't take very long," Luke answered.

Shane rubbed a toe across the fresh dirt just off the patio behind the Strashni compound. Luke had done a hasty job of burying Kara before the sunrise, so the fresh grave was fairly obvious and not very deep. It would work, though, and that was all that mattered.

She would be the first Shane ever turned. Well, technically Luke was her sire, but Shane had given the order.

"What are we going to do about Dimas?" Luke

asked, watching Shane.

"We'll flush him out easily enough," Shane answered, turning back to his friend. "As manipulative as he thought he was, he tipped his hand pretty far. His lust for power makes him easy prey."

"Maybe we should have sided with Theresa, instead of making her our enemy," Luke proposed, folding his arms across his chest.

Shane shook his head. "Nah, you can't make deals with the devil. They always lie." Shane walked back into the compound, Luke following closely. "She would have played nice until the time was right, then betrayed us like Dimas."

They walked down the hallway to their bedrooms. Early morning sunlight was peeking through every now and again, reminding them of the long night they had had. All the other vampires were deep in their death sleep now. Shane knew he wouldn't be too far behind.

"We'll need to establish some rules for the vampires who follow you. And we'll need a bit of a rebrand for the whole tribeless thing." Luke raised an eyebrow.

"Yeah, you're right. I really had just wanted to stick it to Dimas with the whole prophecy thing, but I hadn't really thought through the morning after. I guess I'm the ruler of a bunch of united vampires now." Shane stopped in front of Julianna's room and stared at the door. Neither he nor Luke said anything for a moment.

"Julianna was the one who always believed in you. Who knows how this all might have ended without her?" Luke said, breaking the silence, still staring at the closed door in front of him. "I'd like to honor her memory somehow. Build a memorial or something. Are you okay with that?"

Shane turned to look at Luke with a sad smile.

A flash of a memory played in his mind. He and Julianna when they were kids. He and Julianna when they were teenagers. Him losing Julianna when she became a vampire. Him finding her again only to lose her again. He had made his peace with leaving his human life behind, but suddenly with the heavy weight of losing Julianna again, Shane felt an urge to visit his parents. He placed a hand on Luke's shoulder. "I'd like that, Luke. What a great idea."

Shane opened Julianna's former door slowly and quietly, and then both he and Luke peered in at the sleeping form lying in what was once Julianna's bed. She snored and then rolled over, repositioning herself away from the watchful Shane and Luke. In her sleep, she looked just like a porcelain doll. She was peaceful and innocent-looking.

Shane closed the door again and stared back at Luke, waiting for his snarky comments about bringing her here and putting her up in Julianna's room. They never came.

Luke folded his arms. "So what do we do with the witch?"

"Her name is Camilla," Shane said as response. What more could he say? He didn't really know what they were going to do with her.

"This is no life for her and you know it. She'll never be welcomed or trusted," Luke reasoned.

"Remember when I met you in the basement at Regina's?"

"How could I forget?' Luke laughed. "You were shirtless and clueless, but you could somehow conjure up a fireball."

Shane smiled back. "And you were a wandering gigolo who didn't believe in the Dark Prophecy. But look where we are now."

"I think this little story is just proving that I am usually right," Luke retorted.

"Actually, it's frightening how right you often are." Shane huffed a small laugh. He then turned pensive, staring off over Luke's shoulder, seeing a potential future after the fake prophecy was fulfilled. "I guess what I am trying to say is I'm just as clueless now. Still clueless and conjuring up fireballs, only now I'm somehow in charge. Will you help me?"

Luke snorted. "I thought it was obvious. You're the only tribe I've had in centuries. We're brothers till the end." His eyes turned dark. "But when we find Dimas, I kill him."

Shane nodded. He might use his powers to subdue Dimas, but for everything Dimas had done to Luke over the years, he knew this was the least Luke deserved. "You have my word."

Shane walked to his room and opened the door. "At nightfall, we'll lay out hunting guidelines. Everyone will be hungry, but I can't have a murder spree in Los Angeles. People would notice."

"Would they?" Luke asked, with his cocky, sarcastic smile back on his handsome face.

"Get some sleep," Shane ordered and then closed his door.

He flopped on his bed, tattered clothes from the battle with Theresa still on. His shoulder still smarted a bit, but the pain had mostly subsided. It was definitely a perk of being a vampire. He closed his eyes and he saw Camilla.

Sleep evaded him for a while as he thought through Luke's words. Luke was right about how the vampires would feel about a witch amongst them, but Shane would have to make them trust her.

He envisioned her beautiful face, her smile as he'd carried her back to the compound from the Cascades. The way she made him feel complete.

He would do what he had to in order to ensure her safety and acceptance. His heart depended on it. He had never been one to believe in love at first sight. Hell, he'd never even believed in vampires, and look where that got him.

He fell asleep with the realization both comforting and frightening him.

He was in love with a witch.

†††

Theresa paced back and forth in the warehouse behind her salon. She hadn't gone home yet. She hadn't figured out what to tell Richard. Or should she just kill him and Emily and close this chapter of her life? "Someone make her shut up!"

Elyse ran over to Emily and soothed her. "Shhhh," she urged. Elyse's skin had healed and she once again looked like a beautiful young witch. The potion they had all drunk before the battle—a slightly more powerful version of the watered-down one they had given the betrayer—worked miracles. Every witch looked worn and tired but not mortally harmed in any way. Emily still cried, but her sobs were at least tolerable now. Elyse continued to hold her tight.

"Did they kill Kara?" Emily hiccupped as she asked Theresa, her eyes red and swollen from crying.

Theresa stared at Emily, debating how much of the truth to tell her. She could just lie. Or tell her the truth and then wipe her memory clean later with a spell. Or just kill her now.

All the Harbor Coven witches were gathered in the warehouse, but no one dared answer Emily without Theresa's consent. A heaviness hung in the air as everyone watched and waited to see what she would say.

Theresa thought about the life she'd built with Richard. It had taken her centuries to create her dream life. Handsome, rich husband. A wife and mother. She'd even enjoyed cooking them dinner every day. And in one night, the whole thing had come crashing down. She fumed. Like steam being let out of a kettle, her anger was going to burst, so she kicked a chair that was not too far from her feet. It slid across the room. When it finished sliding, she composed herself and turned to her stepdaughter.

"Worse." Theresa's face twisted into a sneer. "Death is peaceful. It's natural. They turned Kara into a monster. In a few days, she'll be eating human flesh and drinking human blood. When she resurrects, she'll be a vampire."

Emily stared blankly at her stepmother, Elyse still holding her and patting her hair. "But how is that possible?"

Theresa sighed, exasperated. They just *had* to turn the good daughter and leave her with this empty vessel, didn't they? "They're vampires. We're witches. Try to keep up, will you?"

"What do we do now, Theresa?" Elyse asked. Emily, for once, was blissfully quiet.

"What we've always done. Regroup, plan, attack again when they least expect it." Theresa walked over to Elyse and yanked Emily from her arms. "Now if you'll excuse me, I have a family emergency I have to attend to."

"Can't you save Kara?" Emily looked up at Theresa with wide eyes. Theresa was thankful, at the very least, that they were dry and she wasn't blubbering.

Theresa's tone softened. Her heart even squeezed a bit. She had genuinely cared for Kara. "She's past saving now, Emily. The best we could do for her now would be to kill her."

Emily's lip quivered, but to her credit she didn't cry. "Does dad know you're a witch?"

Theresa shook her head. "He knows nothing and for his own sake, we should probably keep it that way. Help me come up with a cover story. And then you have to stick to it." She stuck a pointed finger in Emily's face. "If you don't, I'll have to wipe your memory...or worse."

Emily began to nod her head when the sound of the red door opening and slamming shut pulled everyone's attention.

Theresa's blood began to boil as she recognized the lanky figure of the almost-albino betrayer of the vampires.

Loosening her grip on Emily, she stood up straight and crossed her arms. "You're not welcome here. Be gone. You've caused me enough grief already."

He looked Theresa up and down with judgment all over his face as he continued crossing the warehouse toward the coven of witches. She knew she looked more disheveled and weary than he was used to seeing her. And if he hadn't taken that potion, she'd have turned him to a pile of ash right where he stood.

He was dragging a sack along the floor behind him. It appeared heavy and Theresa was surprised his little skinny arms could actually pull whatever it was.

The betrayer smiled. "You look terrible. Didn't go well with the vampires, I suppose?" He smiled but continued before Theresa could retort. "No matter. I have a present for you." He dropped the top of the sack he'd been pulling, and a blonde head came rolling out of it. He rolled it back in the sack with his foot, still smiling all the while. Emily gasped at the sight.

"Shane's sister," Theresa whispered in complete shock. "She's dead?"

"Ah, well, you and I both know it's hard to be dead when you're already undead." Dimas tucked a lock of long white hair back behind his ear, grinning all the while like a deadly crocodile.

Theresa was sick of his games and she fought the urge to smack the smile right off his wretched, pale face.

"Get out of my warehouse. I lost a family member tonight and I don't have time to play guessing games with you." She grabbed Emily and started walking toward the exit.

"But don't you see? This is your chance at revenge." Dimas gestured at the sack that lay at his feet.

"You've already killed her, you idiot." Theresa continued walking. It had been a long night and she knew she had to brace herself for the day ahead. She still wasn't entirely sure what she was going to do with Richard.

"Bring her back to life," Dimas called. "Aren't you one of the most powerful witches on earth?"

Theresa turned back to the betrayer. "Necromancy? Are you mad?"

"He took something from you and humiliated you. He took everything from me and humiliated me. This is our chance to get even," Dimas sneered, his evil thoughts twisting his ugly little mouth.

Elyse stepped forward. "We could use her, Theresa. If we can bring her back and *control* her, she could get close to him for us. Shane has Kara. We'll have his sister."

Theresa looked at Elyse, staring into her eyes for a long time. She saw a weariness there. She then looked at all her witches, haggard, tired, defeated.

Theresa realized she wasn't the only one who'd lost tonight. Her coven had risked everything for her and come home with their tails between their legs. She had failed them. And in the grand scheme of her life, hadn't her coven always meant more to her than anything?

"You realize that necromancy comes with a steep price. Everything in nature must balance out." Theresa spoke to her coven, looking every witch in the eye. "Are you willing to pay it, witches?"

Elyse stole a glance at the sack at Dimas's feet. "I am."

The other witches murmured their consent, as well.

But it was Emily that really surprised Theresa.

She stepped to Theresa's side with a boldness she had never shown before. "Let's use this vampire bitch to get even with those bloodsuckers."

Theresa smiled at her stepdaughter. Perhaps there was hope for her after all. Watching her sister be drained of blood seemed to have ignited a spark in the teenage girl.

Turning to Dimas, Theresa said, "Well you heard my coven. We're in. What are your demands?"

Dimas folded his arms across his chest and smiled with fangs extended. "Luke and Shane are mine. No one kills them but me."

To Be Continued in Book 2: Vengeance of the Damned

Camilla risked it all to devote herself to Shane, but in the world of Witches versus Vampires, perhaps it's Shane who is taking the bigger risk. What if she is just a plant by Theresa, after all? And on top of everything, it seems there is more to the Prophecy than he'd been told. So now he must begin a new life as the leader of the united vampires even as he awaits the inevitable attack of Theresa and her coven. Find out who comes out on top in Book 2 of The Dark Prophecy trilogy.